MW01170493

Advance praise for *Appearance of Counsel* !

"In *Appearance of Counsel,* Andrew McAleer has written a marvelous Boston crime novel focusing on attorney Joe Gleason and both his family and friends around him. There's more than a little of the late George V. Higgins in McAleer's prose and dialogue, to the point that you may sometimes wonder whether you're reading a book or eavesdropping in a gritty, blue-collar tavern. A quirky and fascinating debut."

— Jeremiah Healy
author of *Spiral* and *The Only Good Lawyer*

"*Appearance of Counsel* is entirely compelling."
— Robert B. Parker

"Andrew McAleer has IT – and that includes, great pacing, dialogue, characters. Long may he labor in this vineyard."
— Gregory Mcdonald

About Appearance of Counsel

SMALL-TOWN lawyer Joe Gleason wants to start a family and get ahead without selling out to the blue blood law firms of Boston.

The young attorney's plan to escape the low reaches of surrogate justice, however, is shattered when a local contractor retains him for a routine collection case that ultimately escalates to murder.

Things become even more complicated for Gleason when Boston detectives Jack Mundi and Reva Smith begin to unravel another mystery: that of a lower echelon mobster contracted by a Beacon Hill lawmaker to smuggle a handgun into the Cambridge Superior Courthouse.

When the good stand up to people of design, untimely death may just be a matter of when. . .

About the Author

Andrew McAleer was born in Boston, in 1967, and took a *Bachelors* in Philosophy and English Literature from Boston College and a *Juris Doctor* from Massachusetts School of Law at Andover. He has contributed to numerous crime fiction journals including *Mystery Scene*, *Mystery Time*, and *The Baker Street Dispatch*. His essays about law and lawyers include a critical analysis of the Lizzie Borden Grand Jury and the History of Suffolk Law School. In addition to being an editor of the *Rex Stout Journal* Mr. McAleer practices law privately in Lexington, Massachusetts, and is a vice president of the Boston Authors Club. He is also an adjunct professor of law at Bay State College in Boston. This is his first novel.

APPEARANCE
OF COUNSEL

ANDREW MCALEER

Protea Publishing
At;anta, Georgia, USA

Title: Appearance Of Counsel
Subtitle: A Suspense Mystery of Boston
Author: Andrew McAleer

Protea Publishing
Atlanta, Georgia, USA

email: kaolink@msn.com
website: www.proteapublishing.com
web page: www.proteapublishing.com/counsel.htm

ISBN 1-883707-72-2 soft cover

ISBN 1-883707-26-9 hardcover

Library of Congress Card Number: 00-111465

Dedication

For my mother and father
and my philosophy professor
at Boston College Stuart Martin.

Acknowledgements

I would like to thank the following: Margaret DiCanio, Peter Lovesey, Katherine Hall Page, Walter Wager, John Shepphird, Evelyn Wolfson, Jacques Barzun, Charles Everitt, Linda Hutton, Norman Connolly, Esq., Leonard Henson, Esq., John Broussard, Joe Delaney, Phyllis Lindsay, Bob Goldsborough, Charles Burns, Kelly Lawrence, Andy Thurnauer, Kate Mattes, Jean Quinn-Manzo, Dennis Lehane, Karen Cord Taylor, Vincent Massey, Assistant AG, Daniel Flaherty, Assistant DA, and the best private detective in the business, Matt Breslin.

ONE

ATTORNEY JOSEPH C. Gleason was pressed against his wife, staring at a hanging mirror above the foot of his bed.

The mirror reflected a black and white portrait of James Cagney being shunted off to the electric chair by a prison guard.

Maria Gleason looked at her husband and said, "I don't like that poster. I don't like the way he stares down at us."

"Angels with Dirty Faces," Joe said. "One of Cagney's best. I can't take it down. He's been hanging there long before you were even a thought in my mind."

"As if I am now."

"More than you know."

"More than Cagney?"

"Much more."

"What a guy." Maria looked into the mirror and saw Cagney's slate countenance in perpetual fixation over them. "It just seems strange a criminal being carted off to his death watching us all the time. Doesn't it ever bother you?"

Joe shook his head. "Nope. I don't see death; I see life. In that picture Cagney will always be alive. Frozen in time. Take it down and bad things might happen. Besides, I've had it up there since high school."

"Frozen in time," Maria said. "Now I know where you get it from. I should've known better than to marry someone half Irish and half Italian. A hybrid of God's two most arrogant creations."

11

From a table radio Boston radio personality Wally Brine was itemizing the incontrovertible facts behind the curse of the Bambino.

"I'm only a quarter Italian," Joe said, "and I'm not arrogant. Just adamant."

"Firm is more like it." Maria folded her right leg up to her navel and removed his boxer shorts with her big toe. "I could have sworn you were at least half," she said before disappearing under the thick comforter.

Joe was in no position to argue.

Afterward.

"Joe?"

"Yeah."

"Why do you have a Canadian flag license plate on your car?"

"Bobby Orr's from Canada."

As if that explained it.

"I still don't have you figured."

"Simple," Joe said, "I'm a dreamer with a men's regular."

BOSTON

IN THE SQUAD room Detective Reva Smith stood with her right shoulder propped against an oak doorjamb. She could hear Otis Reading whistling in the background. "This whole city is like a tennis match and we're the net. They need us to serve, but to them we're just the net."

"Get used to it, Detective. That's the way it's always been," Detective Jack Mundi said. "Some days you're the pigeon and some days you're the statue."

"No. Times have changed," Smith said. "The only things you needed to get by in the 60s were sex, booze, and gasoline."

"You left out cigarettes, general stores, and convertibles," Mundi said. "Besides, you weren't even born till '72."

"I'm wise beyond my years."

"Maybe. But I think you have some things to learn about what you already know."

The departmental diplomat approached. "What's the problem, folks?"

A pause.

Smith and Mundi communicated.

"!"

"?"

"You know the Beatles' song 'Rocky Raccoon'?" Smith said.

"I'm not unfamiliar with it."

"You like to qualify your statements, don't you?" Mundi said to the departmental diplomat.

"Not always," he said. "Go on, Reva."

"Well, Mundi says that Rocky dies at the end, and I say he lives."

A short hesitation.

"I see," the departmental diplomat said with his right index finger abutting his cleft chin. "I'll have to think about that one and give you an answer in the morning if that's okay." He elevated his eyebrows. "Okay, folks?"

"I can live with that," Smith said.

"Okay," Mundi said. "But I don't like this tomorrow business."

❖

HARVARD YARD
CAMBRIDGE, MASSACHUSETTS

IN THE YARD, two men arranged themselves on the steps of Widener Library until their eyes were level. The dark man with wire-rimmed glasses was State Senator Richard J. Custance. His hands pumped inside the front pockets of his topcoat. A tremor ran down his face.

"What I need," he said to the Big Man opposite him, "is to get something cold inside a courthouse. I want to see if you can arrange it for me without any assistance from the inside."

"Please remove your hands from your pockets," the Big Man said. "Cambridge Courthouse?" The velvet collar of his Chesterfield eclipsed the lines of his jaw.

"Right," the Beacon Hill lawmaker said. "The Cambridge Superior. How'd you know?" He lost hold of the Big Man's eyes.

"I follow the news and remember faces. What did you think?" the Big Man said. "I can do that. But it'll cost you—quite a chunk."

A pause for thought. "Which, in real money, means what?"

The Big Man's eyes were hooded but quick and alert. The Senator couldn't make out their color.

"Sixty thousand's reasonable. Reasonable only because I know why you want it. I'd get a hundred, because this is good copy, and after it goes down, it'll never work again. Not around here, anyway. You'll get caught, but you know that. You've thought this out."

The Senator looked away before answering. His

14

eyes grew warm. Then he spoke. "Okay. What do I need to do?"

"Just get the money. I'll be in touch to see if you got it. The sixty in front, and when it's delivered to you inside, you're on your own. Be careful about how you put it together. I don't mind a few hundreds and fifties as long as they're new. I want all the bills new. I don't like to carry used money. Just don't get it all from one source."

"I understand."

"Good."

There was a moment of silence between the contracting parties. Then the Senator spoke again, "Okay. What else do I do?"

The Big Man shook his head. "Nothing. I'll give you five days out when I want it. Have it ready. Case probably won't be marked up for trial until some time in January, so I'd just sit tight if I were you," he said, moving in closer to the Senator. "But remember now, we're locked. It'll be there, and I want you there to collect it. It's in the little things that people tend to fail me."

He put a gloved hand around the Senator's waist and directed him down to the bottom of the granite treads.

Senator Custance stood where he was for a moment before leaving, not quite sure why the meeting had ended. It had happened so fast. He felt a long way from Beacon Hill.

The Big Man looked around the Yard and, with a steady gait, started walking toward Harvard Square. He stopped outside Hollis Hall South when he saw two students wearing nothing but their boxer shorts run out into the November cold and take turns dousing their heads

15

under a wooden water pump. The Big Man watched the scene with some amusement. He flipped open his mobile telephone and placed a call. When a voice answered the Big Man said, "It's me. Put me down for a dime that the death penalty will get pushed through the Senate."

Descending into the subway, the Big Man smiled to himself and wished he'd gone to college.

TWO

TRIAL COURT OF THE COMMONWEALTH DISTRICT COURT DEPARTMENT, DEDHAM DIVISION DEDHAM, MASSACHUSETTS

IF YOU WANT to settle, prepare for trial.

Attorney Joseph C. Gleason met with the prosecutor at pretrial conference and got nothing but shrugs.

At the arraignment, a date for pretrial was set, and at pretrial, a date for a hearing on motions was set. In addition to putting together an eighteen-page Defendant's Omnibus Motion For Discovery, which he cut and pasted from one he had copied during his apprentice days at Cutter & Dudley, he filed a Defendant's Motion To Dismiss, Defendant's Motion for Pretrial Probation, Defendant's Motion To Suppress Statements with the defendant's supporting affidavit, and a Defendant's Motion For Promises, Rewards, and Inducements. Aside from moral grounds, the motions all were on soft footing.

As Joe Gleason climbed onto Route 128 South with his blue 1976 Impala, he was tuning in U2's hit, "Pride." From Route 128 South, Exit 16A hooked the driver onto Route 109 East, and he followed it until taking a right turn onto High Street.

On Pearl Street he was lucky enough to find a space willing to consume his large four-door. Before feeding the meter, he consulted his wristwatch and knew without a doubt his client would be late. Reaching into the glove compartment, he pressed a button, and the back trunk began to yawn. There he found a tie, and when he was done massaging the knot, he fed the meter.

An elderly woman, tugging her mongrel, stopped in front of Gleason's car and pointed to his front license plate.

"What's with the Canadian flag license plate?" she asked.

It wasn't the first time the question had been put to the young attorney. "Bobby Orr's from Canada," he answered.

The woman accepted that as a logical response and then tugged the mongrel's leash. Valuable meter time wasted.

THE DAY WAS becoming clear, but the ground was still wet from heavy morning showers. Gleason hoofed it down Pearl Street, crossed over High Street, passed the Superior Court—where Sacco and Vanzetti were tried—and walked a block over to the Dedham District Court.

When he was at the top of the stairs, a security officer working the metal detector said to a guy in painter's pants, "Everything. Cell phones, beepers, keys, pens, cigarettes, lighters. Everything outta your pockets. Dump 'em out into the dish."

She was ready for Gleason. "Just your bo-bo card, Counselor."

Gleason showed his bar card (bo-bo card) to her and walked through the detector, which sounded his entry. The officer just waved the annoyance away. "Go on, Counselor."

GLEASON MET HIS client outside the probation office

and told her to sit tight while he talked to the prosecutor.

"I can't go to jail," said his client. "I gotta work. I
just want to get this thing ova."

"All right. Listen, I've worked hard on this. I don't
think you have a shot at pretrial probation, but I'll try to
get it continued without a finding, which means if you
plea to sufficient facts and save the state the expense of
a trial, then they'll withhold a finding of guilty and dismiss the charges if you don't get into trouble for the next
year—maybe two years. Remember we went over this?"

His client nodded more out of trust than under-
standing. "I just want this to be ova."

"Okay," Gleason said. "Sit tight while I meet with
the prosecutor."

Gleason walked passed a door bearing the inscrip-
tion SWITCHBOARD and let himself into the prosecutor's den. A fellow who hadn't changed his hairstyle since
his first orientation at the Belmont Hill Day School gave
him something between a frown and a nod — the prosecutor.

"We may not hear all these motions today," the
prosecutor said. "We have a slow judge."

"So what do you want to do?" Gleason asked.

"What do you want?"

"I want exactly what I wanted last time. Pretrial
probation."

The prosecutor shook it off. Gleason knew he
wouldn't get the pretrial probation and just threw it out
there to salt the record.

Gleason said, "All right. Plea to a lesser charge.
Drop the dangerous weapon, continue the assault and

battery, and I'll talk with my client."

The prosecutor reached behind his back, scratched it with the tip of his pen, and then made a face intended to show just how much he'd dealt with. "What was the weapon again?"

"Phone," Gleason said.

"Alcohol in the mix?"

"His and hers."

Another frown. "Best I can do on a domestic is recommend we continue it," the prosecutor said. "But she has to plea to the assault and battery with a dangerous weapon. Otherwise, we hear your frivolous motions and go to trial."

Gleason reached down to pull up one of his socks. The prosecutor's eyes followed his movements.

"Where'd you get those?" the prosecutor said.

"Get what?"

"Those rubbers."

"They're my father's," Gleason said.

"Those are sharp. They don't cover the whole shoe."

"No. Just the sole, heel, and toe. They don't climb all the way up the tongue. I like them because they're discrete and easy to put on."

"Yeah. Those are sharp. What kind are they?"

Gleason lifted his left foot and hitched it onto his right knee while the prosecutor leaned in to read the sole of the rubber.

"Tingley," he said, reading the brand name. "Where'd your father get them?"

"Somewhere up the Burlington Mall. I'll ask him for you."

The prosecutor leaned back and scratched his back again with the tip of his pen before exhaling through his nose. He fanned out Gleason's motions with an aristocratic hand, looked at them for the first time, and then tucked them back into his file.

"You billing the bubble on this?"

"Yeah," Gleason said. "I filed my appearance so I'm stuck with it."

"Once the pink part's in, you're in for the full ride."

Gleason let himself get educated.

"All right," the prosecutor said, "let's see if the people for the Commonwealth can put a smiley face on this today. Continue it as an A and B. Drop the dangerous weapon."

"I'll talk to my client," Gleason said.

His client took the plea and the judge gave it a bang after hearing the prosecutor's recommendation.

Back in his Impala, Gleason looked into his review mirror and tightened his tie. By the time he swung onto the Yankee Division Highway heading north, Dickie Betts of the Allman Brothers Band was picking away at "Blue Sky," and Gleason's tie was in the back seat next to a set of hockey skates. His client was going to pay his fee once she got over the hump.

If you want to settle, prepare for trial. If you want to get paid, get it up front.

❖

JOE GLEASON WAS in a hurry to get out the door that morning when his father, Anthony, stopped him.

"It was raining hard a while ago," he said. "You want my rubbers?"

21

"Thanks, but I have a tough case this morning. I can't worry about getting my feet wet."

Mr. Gleason ignored him and took his rubbers out from the front hall closet.

"Take them. Your shoes need to be resoled as it is. Remember what JFK said: 'There are four ways to judge a man: his house, his car, his wife, and his shoes.' No sense in making yours any worse."

Gleason took the rubbers and donned them half smile and half scowl. What he needed was a good plea for his client, not words of wisdom from John Fitzgerald Kennedy. What the hell could he do?

THREE

BRICK VILLAGE,
ARLINGTON, MASSACHUSETTS

IT WAS QUARTER past eleven in the morning when Tick Dillon walked into Belino's Diner and ordered. "Small tea—cream—three sugars."

The young Italian woman waited for him to catch her smile before dropping the cream into the cup. She liked his brogue despite what she'd heard about Irishmen.

In his van Tick removed two pieces of buttered scali bread from a plastic shopping bag, placed one slice on each knee, and stacked his breakfast sandwich with two slices of orange cheese and bacon-flavored potato chips. The Cranberries' track, "Free to Decide," was coming through the single speaker jerry-rigged to a black wire and resting on a clump of dirty T-shirts and towels on the van's floor.

He was smoking menthol, his attention drawn to a woman in her early thirties humping a tub of laundry, when Attorney Joe Gleason tapped on the driver's-side door. Gleason was holding a coffee and a small wax bag containing two glazed doughnut holes he planned to give to his Labrador retriever, Wags.

Tick rolled down his window and said, "Christ, would you look at that, Joe. She's absolutely fantastic. Fuckin' brilliant like."

"Yeah, three kids and three daddies," Joe said. "You'd be a hot dog in a hallway."

Tick lowered the radio's volume and expelled a cloud of smoke from his mouth.

"She's mighty . . .a perfect hybrid. Looks like the 1950s and porks like the 1970s. She just needs to be properly loved, Joe, is all. Love. Love. Love. Even Christ Himself hung with sinners."

"You're right . . .I'm sorry . . .I forgot above love," Joe said. "It takes a goddamn village."

"Bit cross today, are ya?"

"It's nothin'. Just got stuck washing my hair with soap this morning that's all. Gonna make it in today?"

"After work. I'll give you a shout say half four or so."

"Okay. What do you need, anyway?"

"Just a passport matter, is all. Just need your signature and a stamp. Do you have a stamp, Joe?"

"Yeah. All right, four-thirty," the lawyer said. "Don't leave me hanging." Gleason turned and started walking away.

Dillon filled his mouth with chips and was still chewing when he said, "I won't. I'll be there." He stopped Gleason. "Hey, Joe, I thought lawyers were supposed to wear ties?"

Gleason spun around and showed both palms. "This isn't lawyering, it's nut management. I'll sport a tie when you pricks start paying me."

Tick smiled. He was already turning up the radio. "What she needs is a few good rounds of my famous slap and tickle. Catch you later, Joe."

"Right, Tick. Four-thirty."

Dillon's pager grumbled. It was his boss Jim O'Kane. Instead of answering the page, he lit another cigarette and, while tapping his fingers to Third Eye Blind's "How's it Gonna Be?," watched the woman doing laundry

24

sort her lingerie."

❖

IN HIS LAW office Gleason tossed his dog Wags the glazed doughnut holes and then peeled the label off a banana and affixed it to the plastic frame bordering his computer screen. Next, he read the sports, and a columnist with a double chin observed who should retire, and who missed what play, and then praised some obscure athlete from the good old days. On the front page the governor commented about the upcoming vote in the Senate on the death penalty. "I don't see how Democrats and Senator Custance can stand in the way of this kind of groundswell. The Senate flunked its test earlier in the year, but we have a second chance."

Joe said to himself after tossing the paper, "All about second chances, isn't it, guv?" He leaned. Wags lumbered over and stuffed her nose into Joe's right hand. Her dependent brown eyes looked up at him as if there wasn't a problem he couldn't remedy.

❖

COUNTY KERRY,
IRELAND, 1931
OGLAIGH NA HEIREANN (IRISH REPUBLICAN ARMY) VOLUNTEERS

A man's sins last for three generations.

"ALL NATIONS ARE agreed as to the deserved fate of traitors," the gentleman wearing the derby said while biting on the tip of his London briar pipe. "It has the sanction of God and man."

From a wooden chair in the center of the kitchen,

Michael Sugrue watched nervously as the gentleman with the pipe rolled up his sleeves.

"What is it?" Sugrue asked. "What is it you want me to do?"

"You weren't speaking like a peace-loving nationalist last night, Mickey. You had a fierce mean streak running through you. Now you're shaky."

"It was just talk, is all. I don't want trouble. It was the drink, surely. You know 'twas that."

The gentleman with the pipe removed a photograph from his vest pocket and held it up to his captive.

"Do you know this man?"

"I-I—"

"I say, do you know this man?"

"Yes. I've seen him around recent, sure, but I don't know the man personal."

"His name is Richard McKee from West Belfast. His father worked in exile for a number of years on the potato squads and then earned his freedom.

"He came back over with the English recruits to join the Royal Irish Constabulary. He contributed his services to the military round-ups in '20 by directing them to his former comrades."

"The labor union arrests?"

"Aye."

"What's his boy done?"

"Nothing. But you're going to make him stiff since his old gent up and passed on his own."

"I can't whack him. I don't have it in me."

"But when you do have it in you, you'll act accordingly. It was seen in you last night."

Sugrue moved his head back and forth.

26

"You will do it, Mickey. You people have your fancy farm and have done nothing to show your loyalty to the cause. You'll do it for your family if not for your country."

"No. I'm shaky. You said so yourself. My brother. . .Young Tom. . .He's the one you want. He can do it. He's got powerful, strong hands and a killer instinct."

"Tomorrow," the gentleman with the pipe said. "I don't care who does it. And hereafter, mind your tongue when you take the drink."

"I'll have a talk with Young Tom. He won't let you down."

The man who had been drinking with Michael Sugrue the night before stepped out from behind the man with the pipe and said, "Any man who would sell out his own brother is going to live a long death, Mickey." He backhanded the prisoner on the bone of his cheek. Sugrue's cheek bifurcated, and blood oozed. A warm stream flowed past his gullet and went on to thread his pectoral muscles. The bloodline thinned and dried out before reaching his naval.

❖

BRICK VILLAGE,
EAST END,
ARLINGTON,
MASSACHUSETTS, 1933

YOUNG TOM SUGRUE picked up a sixteen-pound sledgehammer and, without a grunt, knocked down the outside wall to the second-story bathroom of the home he'd been saving for since he fled Ireland. Afterward, he lifted the cast iron tub and tossed it through the demolition.

Outside, he dragged the tub to the backyard and, on the border of his land, dug a three-foot hole, lowered the tub in vertically, and filled in the cavities around it, leaving the top half exposed. He whistled for his dog, Collie, and together, they walked over Mount Independence to Luongo's Nursery, where he purchased a small statue of the Virgin Mary.

When he arrived back home, he completed the grotto by making a flagstone footing in the tub and, taking care that it was securely in place, put the statue under the white hood of the cast iron. Our Lady of Irish Spring.

❖

PRESENT DAY
BOSTON, MASSACHUSETTS

DETECTIVE SERGEANT JACK Mundi, of the Boston Police force, slid his letter-opener into an envelope and unfolded a sheet of bonded paper from "The Law Offices of Mark A. Brooks and Associates." The letter demanded that Mundi appear at a deposition in February as a possible witness with respect to a client of theirs who had been charged with lewd behavior. The defense attorney's letter reminded Mundi of the seriousness of these charges and advised him that, if he had any questions in the interim, he should not hesitate to call their law offices directly.

Following the departmental procedure that all correspondence be stamped with the date of receipt and photo-statically copied as soon as possible, Mundi got out of his chair and stamped the letter.

While he was copying the document, detective

Reva Smith came up behind him. She was scented with something that was a cross between baby powder and Eternity.

She got Mundi's attention and asked, "What do you say? Eleven by eight and a half, or eight and a half by eleven?"

"Eight and a half by eleven," Mundi said.

Smith nodded with approval.

"What'd you do before you became a cop?" Smith asked.

"Traveled."

"Where?"

"Job to job," Mundi said.

"Bogart Sabrina or Harrison Ford Sabrina?"

Mundi looked at his partner as if it were a silly question and answered, "Bogart."

"Good." More nodding. "Good," she said, and then walked away, taking some, but not all, of her scent with her.

Back at his desk, Mundi crumpled up the original of the letter he'd just copied, lobbed it into the air, and hit the trash bin without touching any rim. Next, he crumpled up the photo- static copy and got it in on a rebound. The envelope that had previously contained the important letter with the important matter was all net.

Not bad for a hacker, he thought. Had he known Smith was a Bogey fan, he might have handled his problem differently.

FOUR

AT THE IRISH Village in Brighton, William McDermott drained his third black pint of the afternoon, landed the glass back onto the bar's lacquered surface, and ran a sleeve across his over indulgent face. He was fitting in comfortably at the lip of the bar with a brunette he'd never seen before.

On the other side of the horseshoe bar, Tick Dillon's boss, Jim O'Kane, got the attention of the bartender. He pointed the tip of his cigarette at the smoke eater recessed in the ceiling and asked, "Can you turn that thing on, Liam?"

"It's already on, Jim," Liam said. "You got more than half the place filled with smokers. What do you expect?"

Jim continued, after jerking his head in the direction of McDermott. "How long has McDermott been here?"

"I'd say since about half two." He leaned over the bar, slighted his head at the brunette with McDermott, and said, "And I say he'll stick it out until Rose gets tired of his rounds."

"Do you know her?" Jim said. "No chance of a ride in it for him, then?"

"Not a chance, Jim. —Are you interested?"

Jim O'Kane looked at the brunette and then studied McDermott, who had just finished stuffing a fistful of bar mix into himself. His lunch.

"No, Liam," Jim said. "No interest in her whatever. Make sure she doesn't get too pissed. She shouldn't go home with McDermott. Not tonight."

"You got something going, Jim?"

Jim didn't answer.

"I'll have another, Liam."

Liam pushed himself off of the waitresses' station and came back with a ginger cordial. Jim O'Kane lit another cigarette. It was Friday afternoon, and he planned to save his buzz for later on in the evening when Tick arrived with the answer.

MARY BOYLE LIFTED her hand off Tick Dillon's chest and wiped a tear off her face with her left index finger. She put her hand back on Tick's chest and then slid it under the comforter. She asked, "Where are you off to tonight?"

Convenient was a nightstand with a package of cigarettes. Dillon reached for one and lit up. One of his hands was behind his head, and the other brought the cigarette to his lips. He exhaled while he talked. "I have some business to take care of this afternoon and then I'm meeting Jim over to The Village."

"Can I meet you there?" He knew she was trying to find his eyes, but he let the orange glow of his cigarette occupy his attention.

"Not tonight, Mary. It wouldn't be a good idea. I have to meet with Joe Gleason beforehand to sort the passport thing out, and I have no idea how long it will take. We'd just miss each other or you'd be stuck alone with Jim."

"You can call me when you're done with Gleason. You don't have to meet me at The Village. You could come back here. I'll get some dinner for us."

"No, thanks just the same. I gotta meet Jim right after I call on Gleason. He'll be waiting for me there."

She reached her hand farther down the sheets and tried to persuade him to stay. Dillon just turned over to the nightstand and dropped his cigarette into the mouth of a Coke can. It hissed on its way out, which was a relief since he hated fire. He shifted around until his body cradled hers. He looked into her eyes. "Look," he said, "it's my passport—it expired, is all. I just need Gleason to seal the papers or whatever it is they do."

"Can they deport you?" Mary asked.

"No. I mean, I imagine they can do anything, but I trust Gleason. He worked with us all through law school and still does on occasion. He can sort it out. It's no bother, really."

"But what if they deport you?"

"They can't. Jim's going to make me a partner soon in his business," he said while splicing his fingers through her dark brown hair. "I miss my family and all, but I can't go back to Mallow with nothing. A fellow I know put thirty thousand down on a two-family and put only ten back into repairs. Then flipped the thing less than two months later for a forty thousand-dollar profit. He's no smarter than I am—the key thing is to get the first house."

Mary climbed on top of him and kissed him on the lips. Tick gently moved her off him.

"Listen, Mary," he said, "it's after four already. I have to get going for my appointment to see Gleason."

Tick sat up in bed and dug his wallet out of the back pocket of his trousers, which he had pulled up from the floor. He found Gleason's card and dialed. Mary stared at the scar just below his kidney, where he had had a type-two melanoma removed.

"Joe Gleason," the voice answered.

"Joe, Tick. I'm held up on a job. I'll be a little late."

"What's a little late? Remember, I'm a family man now."

"Say, five o'clock."

"If I'm not here, I'm getting coffee at Belino's and then getting my haircut. Swing up."

"Right. See ya then."

Tick hung up and deposited Gleason's card on the nightstand.

In his office Gleason smiled to himself about Tick's excuse for being late. He'd practically heard the other shoe drop.

❖

THE LAW OFFICE of Joseph C. Gleason was located in Brick Village of Arlington's East End. His office was known to his friends as the "Visitor's Center."

Brick Village is a place where, nearly a century ago, Jews, Catholics, Italians, and Irish lived together, worked together, ignored prohibition together, fought together, and broke bread together long before legislation dictated they must. The Italians and Jews built it and, with no real plan in mind, the Irish went off to fight the codfish aristocracy—the blue blooded Yankees of Boston, their imaginary enemies.

Across the street from Joe Gleason's law office, there was a long, yellow brick strip plaza, and behind that ran a stretch of black hardtop. The hardtop abutted a defunct Boston and Maine Railroad line, which cut

33

in along the hem of Jackson's Meadow. Gleason would sometimes walk the tracks during lunch down to the bridge where he and Jay Mangino had smoked their first cigarette. Less than two years later—at age twelve—Gleason saw Mangino get struck and killed by an orange Mustang and, later, was at Massachusetts General Hospital when a doctor announced he'd done everything possible. During his walks, Gleason would turn around just before reaching the bridge.

The hard top led to Gleason's law office, and he was walking on it toward his shingle with a hot cup of coffee in his left hand. Kids were playing street hockey, and the ball spit out at Gleason. He stopped the orange ball with his foot, picked it up, looked at it, and hesitated before tossing it to a chubby kid who he figured wouldn't have had a chance to handle the ball otherwise.

The chubby kid's recovery was short lived. Another kid with gleaming sneakers hooked the ball and tucked it into the net the chubby kid was supposed to look out for.

Tick Dillon witnessed the scene while standing outside Gleason's office. "You know, Joe," Tick said, "you often do more harm by trying to help others."

Gleason looked at him for a moment before looking down at his keys. "And they're the ones who usually come back and bite you," he said.

Tick said, "Joe, why do you have a Canadian flag license plate?"

"Came with the car when I bought it. Just never got around to taking it off. Besides, Bobby Orr's from Canada."

Tick let it go over his head.

The law office was a refurbished gate tender's shack

that consisted of about two hundred square feet and was mostly constructed of slow-growth heart pine milled in South Carolina and dumped off by the railroad at the turn of the 19th century. The heart pine forests propagated around the time of the Magna Carta, and by the time the settlers came there were some eighty million acres covering the South. A hundred and fifty years later there were ten thousand acres remaining. The forests were dense and little sunlight could penetrate. With the reduced sunlight, the trees grew only an inch in diameter every thirty years. Slow growth makes the wood harder. Too much sunlight and it grows too quickly, making it soft and weak.

Inside his office Gleason had a small coal stove, which—along with cases of Miller High-Life—attracted a fair number of acquaintances during the winter months.

Gleason's eleven-year-old Labrador, Wags, stood up from her pillow bed and walked over to Tick and gave him a whiff. Tick gave her a rub and Wags returned to her pillow and slumped down after a few loops.

"I don't think she likes me too well," Tick said.

"She's just old," Gleason said. "Probably pissed off that we woke her up from her nap." Gleason extended his arm. "Sit down, Tick."

"Floors are holding up nicely, aren't they?" Tick said.

"Not bad. Had some shit-box floor sander from Brighton in here helping me. Said he had great hands, but it turned out he had lousy thumbs. Then he suckers me into a satin finish because that's all he had in the van for a finish coat."

"Satin brings out the grain. It was all part of the master plan to give you beautiful floors. Besides, I can't guarantee they'd hold up to you parading around in golf spikes now that you're an important solicitor. Look at you; you're already getting a little stomach on you. Nothing to you when you worked the big sander, you fat bastard."

Gleason smiled. He swiveled and played with the window shade behind his desk. He raised it halfway up the window and let go of it slowly, making sure the coils didn't send it spinning. It was starting to rain. Someone outside was clawing the pavement with a metal rake.

The lawyer faced Tick and asked, "So, what do you have, a passport application you need signed?"

Dillon reached over Gleason's desk and spread out an application that, along with his shirt, looked like it had been kept in his wallet.

"Okay," Gleason asked, "what the hell do I do with this thing?"

"I just need you to stamp it," Dillon said, "or whatever it is you fat bastards do."

Gleason ran his eyes over the document. "What the Christ—it's in Spanish."

"It's Gaelic. You're on the wrong side." Dillon reached over the desk and placed a finger the size and shape of a yam on the section Gleason was to fill out. "Right here. And there it says about a stamp or seal. I think I glue my picture there and you stamp it."

"No. I think what I do is just seal it, and then you give the picture to whoever and they seal them in your passport."

Gleason filled out the necessary information and then sealed it with his notary seal.

"Did you sign this thing yet?" Gleason asked.

36

"Sure," Tick said. "My name's right on it above your own."

"Where?"

"Right there."

"Where? … Patrick T. Dillon? That's you?"

"You didn't know my name? After all of four years?"

"Just never thought of it. And when you signed this, it was your free act and deed?"

"Yes, it was, counselor."

"And you're over the age of eighteen?"

"I am."

"And you're of sound, lucid, brilliant mind?"

"I'm fucked in the head like any Irishman."

"Okay, good," Gleason said. "Welcome to our country. All joking aside, Tick, get this thing done—you shouldn't let it expire."

"Can they deport you, Joe, for this?"

"All I remember about immigration is that they can do whatever the hell they want. Will they? I don't know, but don't give the man with the fuzzy nuts anything to hang his hat on, you know?"

"Right. Listen, Joe," Tick said, "I got another problem, and you can charge me for it. A contractor Jim and I worked for is after filing bankruptcy. He had us do some floor work when he knew he didn't have the money."

"I tell you guys you've got to get this stuff in writing. You've got this handshake honor thing going, and before you know it, they've got you bent over sticking it to you up the balloon knot. How much you talking?"

"Three thousand. He kept telling us it was on the

way and then said he'd pay only half and then never paid that. It just went on and on for months."

"Three grand is enough to fight over, but you should've come to me earlier. Bankruptcies are tough to get around. I'd treat you fair, but if a judge gives the bankruptcy a bang, which is likely, you end up with about ten cents on the dollar, and that's only if there's enough money to trickle down to you and if the prick keeps up with his payments. And they almost never do."

Dillon leaned back and lit a cigarette. Jim O'Kane was going to give him half of the three thousand toward making him a partner in his hardwood flooring business if Dillon could collect the debt, and Dillon had figured Gleason would just offer to do it for free. "So you're after saying Jim shouldn't bother then?"

"If he wants me to do a dance on it he can talk to me. I'm just letting you know up front that he's got a fight on his hands. I'd have to figure out how much it would cost me. It sucks, I know, but you guys have to get money up front and at least cover your costs and labor."

"It doesn't seem right that he can just go on and file bankruptcy and get away with it."

"I know. But sometimes if something tastes like shit, you've just got to swallow it all at once, hold your nose, and forget about it. Besides, I'd probably do more harm trying to help."

"You're a brilliant poet, Joe," Tick said. He stood up from his chair. "I'll talk to Jim about it. I'm off to see him now. By the way, what's the difference between a barrister and a solicitor?"

Just as Tick finished letting out the question, the street hockey ball came crashing through one of Gleason's windows. Before Joe shot out of his chair, Tick looked out the door window in time to see the tail end of the chubby kid fade into the brambles along Jackson's Meadow.

"It looks like your little round friend returned the favor. Kids fit in one way or another."

Gleason examined the mess, and then said while looking out at the meadow, "Barristers are usually fatter and have higher cholesterol—the bad kind."

Dillon grinned. "Hey, I'm doing a side job in the morning over to Brookline. I could use a hand."

"I could use the scratch," Gleason said. "I got a window to pay for."

"You need a hand with this?"

"No. You'd do more harm trying to help."

"Cheers," Tick said. "Be at my place at six in the morning then."

"Be there with my spikes on."

FIVE

State Senator Richard J. Custance stood up from his study chair in Concord, Massachusetts, walked over to the heat panel, and raised the heat to eighty degrees. He was shaking.

He poured himself a brandy and sat back down at his desk. In his left hand he held up a small, framed picture of his six-year-old daughter. She was standing in their Boston Whaler docked up in Alton Bay, New Hampshire. She was smiling, her front teeth gone, her life jacket fastened. Far in the background of the picture, he could make out the spine of Alligator Island slightly arched above Lake Winnepesaukee. From a distance, the pine trees looked soft enough to pat.

The Senator placed her picture back onto his desk and thought about Julian Hill—the man who had raped, killed, and mutilated his child.

Hill, a 250 pound recluse, decided one day to swing out to Concord and find a schoolgirl to spend an idle afternoon with. He settled on six-year-old Jackie Custance and, with the promise of a puppy, carted her back to his apartment on Rindge Avenue in Cambridge. She fought. While a portion of the world complained about the wickedness of Teletubbies, Hill turned on the gas jets to his kitchen range, snuffed the flame, and made her inhale until she passed out.

On the living room rug he raped the child. Somewhere during the events—as they were now termed by the Hill defense team—the child suffocated. Afterward, he rolled her up in the rug, folded it, tied it together, and stuffed it into a dumpster.

About two weeks later, in one of the concrete bays of an Allston transfer station, her remains were scooped by a front-end loader.

JIM O'KANE LOOKED at the Ballintine clock hands above the bar and saw that it was just about six o'clock. Time for a warm-up before Tick arrived with word from Gleason. He ordered a pint of Guinness and a double shot of Paddy. Tick had size and strength, but most of all, a temper that was easily prodded by inebriation and loyalty to the wrong people.

The pub was filling up with plasterers and painters, and The Village was only too happy to cash their pay checks at the till since the money was coming right back anyway. O'Kane was having a tough time holding on to the stool he'd been saving for Tick. Through the loud voices he could hear Luke Kelly's version of "The Town I Loved So Well."

McDermott looked across the bar and saw O'Kane toss back the double Irish, and then, before making a visit to the bathroom, went back to the brunette he'd been working on for a quick exchange that made her throw back her head in laughter.

O'Kane ordered two more whiskeys. He saw McDermott make his way to the men's room, but wasn't worried. He couldn't sneak out of the pub via the loo. There was one door in and one door out - for all of them.

By the time Tick Dillon made his way over to Jim O'Kane, he had two pints handed to him. He laid one in front of O'Kane.

"There's your man right there in the washroom,"

O'Kane said.

"Saw him on the way in," Tick answered. "Old boy half in the bag already, is he?"

"He is."

"Does he know you're here?"

"He does. What did Gleason say?"

"Said there's nothing you can do," Tick answered. "Bastard can just not pay you."

O'Kane's eyebrows bumped. He looked over at the men's room door and threw back both shots of Irish.

Liam the bartender said, "Would you like to try another of those?"

"Keep them coming, Liam," O'Kane said. "Fuel to feed the fire."

In the bathroom, McDermott let the cold water run while he urinated. When he returned to the sink, he washed his hands and then the oiliness from his face.

SIX

WITH HIS FORK, the Big Man poked his last bite of rare porterhouse and then looked down at his beagle, which begrudged his owner's every bite. He scraped the piece of steak off the fork back on to the plate and laid it on the carpet for the beagle.

"That's a good boy. Good boy," the Big Man said. After lapping it up, the beagle left the room.

Abandoned, the Big Man made another mobile call. "It's me. Put me down for another dime on the same." He leaned back in his leather recliner with his hands laced and rested his eyes.

JOE GLEASON LIVED in a duplex above his parents on Mount Independence in Arlington, the same home his maternal grandfather, Tom Sugrue, passed papers on in 1933.

He threw in his *Night Moves* CD and heard Bob Seager sing "Ship of Fools." His wife Maria kissed him while he stared, from their bed, at the old light fixture nub fastened to the ceiling.

"Your mother invited us down for dinner," Maria said.

"What do you want to do?"

"I think we should go down."

"You sure?"

"Yeah. You got out late, so she cooked it anyway."

He moved into her, slid his hand up her sweater, and rubbed her stomach. "She's cooking for three more. How's the baby?"

"He asked for you today."

"I don't know why, but I want the first one to be a girl," he said. "I just always wanted a little girl. Just make someone who'll be a good lawyer. I need someone down the office who knows what the hell they're doing."

"It just takes some time," Maria said. "How did things go this morning?"

"Not too bad. I got her a good plea."

"You're a good lawyer. You had guts enough to go out on your own."

"I've never been on my own. I've always had the support. It's just that I'm at the point where I ask myself if it's fair. I mean, I help some people, but who really pays for it? It comes out of my family. I'm no good at asking people for money. Then half the time I'm being put down, I don't even know it."

"You're tired. You have my support, which means you don't get my pity. I think it was Kierkegaard who said that pity is the worst of all sins."

"You don't even go to church except Christmas and Easter. But that's okay, a good friend told me that even Christ Himself hung out with sinners."

Maria punched him lightly in the ribs. She hit his port wine mark.

"I'm just kidding. I know . . . .I know. It's just that I'm losing my fire, that's all." Frustration, with a sprig of self-pity.

"What do you mean? I thought you were Mr. Adamant this morning."

"That was a long time ago. Tick asked me about a case today. I see now it's a loser, but a year ago I would've taken it on. I kinda pushed it away."

"Maybe it's experience. You're able to see the business end of the legal business."

"Yeah, but is that right? In this case I felt weakened by experience. I mean, should it be a business or about helping people who need it? Jim O'Kane got ripped off, and Tick asked me about it. I basically told him Jim's gotta eat it. It's a tough case, but I would've at least fought it a year ago."

"But you probably wouldn't have gotten paid."

"And if I had, I would've felt guilty."

"You'll be a good father," she said.

Joe didn't know how to respond so he pushed it off. "Is my father home, do you know?"

"Yeah, he was in the garden earlier."

"I think I'll go down and visit him in a bit."

They rested for a while, and when Joe finally got up to head downstairs, Bob Seager was singing about being "Down on Main Street."

JOE'S FATHER, ANTHONY Gleason, was in the living room reading the obituaries when Joe came in and sat across from him in an Edwardian rocker. Wags followed him in, stuck her nose in Mr. Gleason's crotch, and then sat down next to Joe.

"Your mother will have a bird if she sees you in that rocker," Anthony Gleason said.

"You're the one with the dirty hands and knees."

"I noticed as I drove by the farm tonight that they tarped the apple bins outside. They do that when there's a frost warning, so I took in the last of the tomatoes."

"Isn't it a bit early for frost?"

"Not really. David O'Sullivan was saying just the other day on his garden show that we've been fortunate.

You can expect a killing frost any time after the eleventh of October. I remember the year Oswald knocked the top off Kennedy's head, we didn't have a killer frost until the day of Kennedy's funeral. The day before, your mother and I had seven lilies bloom. We'll have to put aside a few seeds from the tomatoes I picked today for next year."

"I think I'll get the starters going early this year—maybe January," Joe said.

"Of course, you shouldn't start them too early, *but*," he said shrugging away his own advice, "January might be okay. I remember one year a volunteer started in late September, and I ended up taking it in for the winter. It lasted fine and did just as well as the others," Mr. Gleason said.

"There seems to be an exception for every rule."

"I was reading in the obits today about a fellow I thought you might be interested in—about a judge who graduated from Boston College Law School back in the early 30s. Actually, he started out at Harvard Law and then transferred to Boston College for some reason. It said he worked as a country lawyer and was a great trial lawyer. When the big firms would underestimate him, he'd sneak up on them and catch them flatfooted. Eventually he got himself a judgeship after becoming an officer in World War II."

"That's interesting, because Boston College Law wasn't founded until 1926. It would've been relatively new when he transferred out of Harvard. You'd think he would have stuck with Harvard."

"Just goes to show what you can do," Mr. Gleason said. "No matter where you come from."

Joe's mother, Alice Gleason, called them in for

dinner, and Wags was on the jump.

SEVEN

MIDDLESEX COURT,
SUPERIOR COURTHOUSE,
3RD DISTRICT, CAMBRIDGE

ON THE FOURTEENTH floor of the courthouse, a tall, thin court officer stepped off an elevator leading to the holding cells. In a lunchroom across from the elevator, two court officers were getting in a hand of crazy eights.

The tall court officer walked into the lunchroom and, from a refrigerator that would be more properly termed an ice-box since it was so old, pulled out a processed deli sandwich stored in a disposable black container and grabbed a five-ounce carton of milk.

The officer walked by one door and could hear one of his colleagues doing push-ups in a common office. He was supposed to be watching the surveillance screen, which gave a live video of every room in the courthouse. The screen was broken down into small squares of footage and, at the officer's choosing, could zoom in and enlarge any room in the building to the full size of the screen.

From the large holding cell, two heads with gray, unshaven faces came up to the breathing slit in the red door to see who was walking by. A hand pushed out the empty sandwich cartons stuffed into the slit. One inmate said, "Put me in with the fuckin' skinner. Let me outta here. I won't touch him."

The court officer ignored the request. The prisoner said in response, "Then don't give the fuckin' fat skinner nothin' to eat for supper. No supper for the skinner. No supper for the skinner." The chant was repeated in harmony by the rest of the lock-ups.

A skinner is a child molester, and they have to be in a separate lock-up. If they're in the holding cell with the rest of the holdovers, they'll get killed or badly beaten. When the holding cell starts to get too full, the men in the cell start to ask if they can go into the single cells with the skinner.

"Get back, gentlemen." the court officer said. "He's got a long life ahead." He then slid Julian Hill, the individual accused of destroying Senator Custance's daughter, the sandwich and milk through the service opening of the green bars that enclosed his six-foot-by-six-foot cell.

The court officer turned around and went back to the elevators. He removed some keys from his pocket, selected one, and turned it when he had it in the slot next to the elevator car. When he stepped into the elevator, he turned the key again in the proper slot. The door shut and didn't open until he was in the holding cell behind Courtroom 6B of the Superior Court.

❖

DINNER AT THE GLEASONS'

UNCLE DAN DRANK and so did Margaret.

Mrs. Gleason finally sat down to dinner with the rest of the family after carrying a hot dish of sweet potatoes, sans potholders, to the table. She just shook off the pain and then put two of them onto her father's plate. Her father, Tom Sugrue, was in his eighty-ninth year. He said before each meal, "Bless, bless, oh Lord these gifts upon which we are about to dine, and feed the poor wher-

49

ever they are with Christian bread and wine."

They somehow got on the topic of cooking.

"My Uncle Dan was helpless. He couldn't boil water, and I tell you he was the slowest eater," Mrs. Gleason said. "We'd all want to go out and he'd just sit there with his food. He was a drinker, but boy was he a character. I was his favorite."

"What'd he do?" Joe said.

"Aside from drinking, he was a contractor, and he didn't know what the heck he was doing half the time, but he knew all the—" she waved her hand. "Whoever the people were who got work for the city, and he used to get all the jobs. He ran his business out of the back sun porch. He was what we called a One Parish Gypsy. He could just never settle down. Always had to be on the move around the city, but never left home unless he had to."

"Now, who was he? Your mother's brother?" Joe said.

"Yes. He was the one who made you kids lasagna with cottage cheese when I was in the hospital with my first miscarriage."

"I kinda remember that guy. Did he have any kids?"

"A boy. He was married twice, and my mother gave her the toughest time, but she was a good person."

"Gave who a tough time?"

"His second wife, Margaret. She was the first one I ever knew who came from a single house. Up until then I thought everyone lived up or down."

Joe sipped milk. "Was he in the War?"

"He joined the Navy and told them he was a cook.

He went off with a cookbook my mother got for her wedding."

"Your mother got a cookbook as a wedding gift?" Maria said.

Maria drew a hard look from Mrs. Gleason.

"Vacuum cleaners were too heavy and bulky to wrap back then," Joe said.

"Good point, counselor," Maria said. "I can't wait until Mother's Day."

Mrs. Gleason said, "One time Dan stayed home because he missed his ship and it ended up getting sunk. Everyone was killed."

"Did he get into trouble?"

"For what?"

"For missing his ship," Joe said.

"No, he was in the hospital, sick with a ruptured colon."

"Oh. You made it sound like he missed the ship because he was drunk or something."

"No. Margaret wouldn't let him drink after that," Mrs. Gleason said.

"He drank during the War and well after," Mr. Gleason said.

Mrs. Gleason: "No. I don't think he did."

"Well, he took a cab home from New York once while on leave and spent over two thousand dollars in a week, so he was spending it on something. And then whenever his son from his first marriage showed up in town to play college ball, Dan would watch him play and go off on a toot afterwards."

A stick of soft butter had disappeared during the meal. Mr. Sugrue extended an arm and mopped the butter dish with a tear of brown bread.

Joe offered his mother's father the last of the lamb chops.

Uncle Dan drank and so did Margaret.

EIGHT

JIM O'KANE MADE a face as he swallowed the bile that erupted into the back of his mouth.

"Look at him," Tick said observing McDermott's behavioral cues, "stuffing himself."

"Ya know, Tick?"

"What?"

"It's always news when a royal goes out and gets a new piece of arse. It's not news."

"It's not?"

"No. I'll tell ya what would be news about a royal."

"Tell me, Jim."

Jim's right index finger was pogoing off the bar's hardwood.

"It would be news, Tick, if a royal went out and got a fuckin' job. That would be news."

They drank to it.

Liam the bartender was quick to recharge their glasses.

It was after eleven, and the music was growing louder and harder in Tick's head. O'Kane couldn't handle whiskey and started pacing himself, but kept pushing more and more into Tick, who didn't seem to notice that he was a couple up on his friend.

"What should we do to the bastard?" O'Kane asked. "I can't run a business where people don't pay. You'll hold him down while I hand his fat arse to him."

"He's so pissed he won't feel it."

"Nor remember who did it." O'Kane jerked his

head at the bartender. "Couple more, Liam."

The pub was so loud, Liam was reduced to reading lips, but still didn't a beat.

Tick Dillon was rocking from side to side. The loud music was reaching a crescendo in his head. He kept rolling and unrolling his sleeves. His hands were sweating one minute and the next, were cold and clammy. Neither Tick nor Jim had any interest in the two women who had moved in next to them, waiting for a chance to start up a friendly conversation.

McDermott's brunette was long gone, and he was trying to buddy up with a couple of acquaintances he had ignored while he had the brunette's attention. He was trying to convince them to head out to the Kinvara Pub before the last call rush, but they were happy where they were.

McDermott wasn't as drunk as O'Kane and Dillon thought. Nor was he as drunk as he should have been. On his way to the door, he began to make polite conversation to make his moves less noticeable. O'Kane and Dillon threw back what they had, and both lit cigarettes.

O'Kane was small but scrappy looking. He felt powerful around Dillon and muscled right into the pockets of open space Dillon formed while cutting into the eddies of payday drunkards.

When O'Kane bumped into a hand and the hand spilled some beer on him, he jammed his cigarette into the ear of the hand's owner. When the owner assessed Tick, he recoiled. Jim O'Kane specialized in making snowballs for others to throw.

As McDermott got closer to the door, his smile became more and more forced. His heart was beating, his bladder urgent, and his blood quickened. Someone pushed a beer in front of him, and he just shook it off. When he made it outside, a blast of cold spilled into his open flannel and seemed to fry the sweat off of his chest. It had been a soft, autumn afternoon when he had entered the pub, and now Market Street had given way to raw moisture and darkness.

It was difficult to believe that, on this urban street, lined with franchise banks and all-night drunk stops, a way of life once existed. Even up until the 50s, cows would sometimes escape from the stables at the stockyards and hold up traffic and streetcars, as butchers with bloody smocks would set out on foot to hunt down the animals on their short-lived reprieve. That way of life made it into the Charles River, too. Kids were sometimes lucky enough to spot heads of cattle floating down the river within stick poking distance.

McDermott turned up Market Street and walked at what he thought was a good clip. His eyes followed the sheen of the wet street.

Two bodies stepped outside the pub onto a bluestone slab. The two bodies were very drunk—very angry—and grew just as cold as the dark figure they followed up Market Street.

NEXT DAY JOE walked into the kitchen. At sixty-three, Mrs. Gleason showed no sign of slowing. It was her way of handling two full-term miscarriages.

It was five-thirty in the morning and the coffee she had brewed was getting old. Her father, Tom Sugrue, was at the kitchen table, and in front of him was his morning intake: two boiled eggs, two pieces of toast—the heels—a bowl of cereal, and a cup of tea. He wore a red-checkered flannel shirt buttoned up to his neck.

Mr. Sugrue was round and strong. In 1931, at age twenty, he had immigrated to America from a small village in County Kerry, Ireland, called Cahirciveen. A year later, he had sent for his wife and baby girl, Alice, Joe's mother.

"Why are you up so early?" Mrs. Gleason asked Joe.

"I'm doing some floor work."

"No work today?" Joe's grandfather said. He slurped his tea.

"I'm working floors today, Grampie."

"There is nothing for nothing in this world," Mr. Sugrue said. "Man must work with the sweat of his brow to earn his bread."

Mrs. Gleason held up the coffee pot. "Want a cup of coffee?"

"I'll just grab one down at Belino's."

"I don't know why you people have to go out and buy your coffee when you can have it here."

"It just becomes part of your day."

Mrs. Gleason cranked open the window in front of the kitchen sink and tossed out some moldy bread for the birds. Any stale bread went to her father.

"Can you watch Wags this morning, Mom? Maria won't be around to walk her."

"I'm having my hair done at eight." Joe showed his disappointment. "I'll work it out with your father."

"Thanks, Mom." Joe patted his grandfather on the back. "I'll see you, Gramp. Don't work too hard."

"Sometimes knowing you'll never finish is what keeps you going," his grandfather offered.

DETECTIVE REVA SMITH squared off a few pages on Jack Mundi's desk and, although they were still a bit disheveled, she stapled them together.

"You know," she said, "I heard something funny. Sick, really. People are starting to put down buckets of cash that the death penalty will get pushed through."

Detective Mundi looked up at her and asked, "It'll never fly with Custance opposing it. By the way, what do you like better, the first part or the last part of 'Layla'?"

"The back nine," Smith answered. "Springsteen's 'Blinded by the Light' or Manfred Man's?"

"Springsteen's," Mundi said.

Smith nodded and then walked away, taking some, but not all, of her scent with her.

Mundi nodded to himself and said, "A true Eric Clapton fan. And Springsteen. Wish I'd known that before this G-D mess."

❖

JOE GLEASON SAT tipped against the white panel of a garage door in Brookline. The garage belonged to a huge brick house that was the original site of Gordon College. He had taken off his kneepads, and his sweat had seeped through his jeans around the knees. It was cold, but the fresh air was a fair exchange from the floor sanding dust. He was massaging an orange in his hands.

"Having a tough time at it today, are ya?" Tick said.

"Yeah," Gleason said, "I wish I could lose weight as fast as I lose my talents."

Tick Dillon was standing in front of Gleason. After gulping half his Gatorade, he took out two slices of buttered bread from a plastic shopping bag. With his teeth, he tore open a bag of cheese and onion chips and emptied a healthy portion of them onto the slices of bread. While chewing, he looked down at Gleason with some confusion. Still masticating, he asked, "What are you doing to that there, Joe?"

"Squeezing the orange," Gleason said. "If you keep squeezing it, it makes it easier to peel."

"I'll have to try it."

"I've never seen you touch a piece of fruit since I met you."

"It's tough to get to the market. You come home and you're too tired from the day's activities to do anything. I always end up grabbing a sub or fast food for dinner. It's expensive, too. Much cheaper to go the market, isn't it?"

"Yeah. I mean, I can't afford to eat out every day. You figure a sub's about five bucks, a Coke a buck, and chips a buck. It costs you about seven bucks for lunch. That's thirty-five a week and that's not including coffee every morning. That's another buck at least. And then they want a tip on top of that. You could save about two bills a month just bringing your lunch."

"You feel terrible after it, too," Tick said. "I've got six thousand saved. What do you reckon I should do with it?"

"You could put some in the market. Something safe and just let it grow."

"You could lose it, though, in the market, couldn't you?" Tick said.

"Sure, you could keep it in a sock with your first communion money, but if you want to take a chance and start your own business, you've got to do something more than just leave it in the bank. That's the Irish way. Play it safe. Just sock it away."

Tick smiled. "It reminds me of Paddy Tighe. All over everyone felt bad for him. He'd just walk around with rags for clothes and everyone would feed him and buy him drinks. The whole village took care of him. He was in his eighties when the angels touched his shoulder. When they cleaned out his cottage, they found an old rubber boot under his bed full of money—tens and thousands of pounds. I guess I'm a Paddy Tighe. I'll just keep saving and not take my chances with the market. I have to get that first house. That's the key."

Joe Gleason looked at his watch. "I should've brought this orange inside before break instead of leaving it in the van. It's all cold and it's killing my teeth. I hate that."

Tick finished his Gatorade and then mashed a few potato chip crumbs into the driveway with the tip of his boot.

"Talk to O'Kane about that bankruptcy matter," Gleason said.

Dillon waved his hand away. "He's not gonna bother. By the time you chase it down, it would end up costing him money."

Tick's delivery was slow. His eyes were puffy.

"You booze hard last night?" Gleason asked.

"I touched my pillow and the next thing you're waking me. I didn't drink much, but I didn't eat anything."

"That'll do it," Gleason said. "Well, let's get back. We're on our own clock."

"Right," Dillon said, and then lit a cigarette.

Gleason put on his dust mask and went back inside the house. He didn't bother with his kneepads. They were too wet and cold.

NINE

AFTER WORKING WITH Tick for most of the day, Joe Gleason turned down a beer and went to his office. There was a message on his voice mail from his mother. He called home, and his grandfather answered.

"Hello?" Mr. Sugrue shouted.

"Grampie. . .It's Joe. . .Get my mother."

"Hello?" a louder shout.

"It's Joe, Grampie. Can you get my mother?"

"No work today?"

Mrs. Gleason took the phone from her father.

"Mom. It's Joe. What happened?"

"You know," she said, "you almost lost your dog this afternoon."

"What happened?"

"He got up when he saw that old blue car coming up the street and started to follow it. He must have thought it was your car."

To Mrs. Gleason all dogs were "he's."

"Wasn't she tied up?"

"You never tie him."

"That's because she always stays with me."

"Well, like I said, he thought it was your car so he started to follow it. He's okay now. I have him out front with some chicken bones your grandfather tossed him."

"Chicken bones? I'll be home in a bit."

It wasn't the first time they had had this conversation.

Tom Sugrue was at the end of the Gleasons' driveway leaning on a black walking stick when Joe pulled out front and parked.

His grandfather said to him, "No work today?"

"I'm working. I just came home to get the dog."

Mr. Sugrue started. "There are no snakes in Ireland, but I've seen some since I've come here. But I have seen more sneaks than snakes."

Joe half listened and then took Wags, who had already made quick work of the chicken bones, inside.

When he came back outside, his grandfather was sitting in the front seat of his car.

THE DEPARTMENTAL PAIN-in-the-ass came up and spoke to Detective Reva Smith. She was hung over and had already used up two cigarette breaks.

"Detective," the departmental pain-in-the-ass said, "these reports aren't in order."

Smith stood up, pointed a finger at him, and said, "Shut your fucking trap."

The departmental pain-in-the-ass shrugged, humphed, and began taking his departure. Smith stopped him.

"And another thing. If I ever hear you make another Stevie Wonder or Helen Keller joke, I'm gonna drag you outside by your nuts and knock your fucking block off."

The departmental pain-in-the-ass shrugged and walked away.

He didn't bring his problems to work. And everybody knew it, too.

AT TWENTY MINUTES past one in the morning, the

Gleasons' telephone rang.

After two rings, Maria scooped the receiver. "Hello?" The voice on the other end muttered something. She handed it to Joe. "One of your drunk friends. I think it's Tony."

"Hello?" Gleason said.

"Gleason," Tony yelled. "I'm drunk outta my tits."

"Where are you?"

"I'm at the police station."

"Listen, keep your mouth shut."

A police officer took the phone from Tony.

"Joe, it's Brian. He's not at the station. We're down outside the Stone Store on four corners. He's tanked. I can't let him drive, but this is as far as I'll carry him. The drunk shuttle ends here."

"I'll be right down, Brian. Thanks."

"What's wrong?" Maria asked after Joe had hung up.

"Tony's pickled and Brian's gonna have to bust him if I don't get down to the four corners and pick him up."

Brian the cop got out of his cruiser and adjusted his black leather jacket when Gleason pulled up to the Concord Hill Market, known to the locals as the "Stone Store."

"What happened, Brian?" Gleason said.

"Fuckin' kid was burning down the Mystic Parkway spilling cobblestones all over the place. He would've ended up in the river if I hadn't stopped him."

"Giving you a hard time?"

"I told him to leave his truck and that I'd drive him home, and when I got him in the cruiser, he starts going

63

bananas, trying to reach for my gun."

"Good thing he didn't try reaching for your wallet."

"I almost had to call it in. He started screaming for you, so I gave him one more chance. I'm off the drinking rotation, Joe. I can't be a cop and a friend to these guys much longer. They're starting to think they got a license to drink and drive. Pile of assholes is what they are."

Gleason looked over at the cruiser and saw Tony slumping with his face pressed against the rear driver's-side window. He asked, "What, is he passed out now?"

"Yeah. You gotta get him out of here."

Tony Vaccaro's head was bobbing in the passenger's seat of Joe's car. His tongue was hanging out. Joe woke him up so he wouldn't bite it off with his teeth.

"Wake up, Tony."

"I'm up, for Christ's sake. Don't take me home," Vaccaro said.

"It's almost three o'clock. Where am I supposed to take you?"

"I can't go home like this. Take me to your office."

"I don't have any beer there."

"Yes, you do."

"Well you're not getting any. I'll make you a coffee and that's it. If you want to sleep there, you can, but I'm taking the beer."

Tony exhaled. "Everything's changing."

"Fewer people to drink with. That's not change, that's the way it always happens; little by little. Not fast enough. Just look around. The guys ten years older than

64

us are all drinking O'Douls, talking about their first wives and how happy they are to be free."

❖

Gleason brewed some coffee in his office bathroom and came out with a cup for himself and Vaccaro.

"So what the hell set you off?"

"Nothing," Tony said.

"That's what I suspected. Nothing."

"I don't know. I have a good business. It's just a rat race. A mother fucking rat race that goes seven days a week and there's just no let-up, man. I just see guys out there who don't have a clue, and everything seems to fall into place for them. Then before you know it you're old and some doctor's slipping on a glove telling you to stay out of the sun and you're rolling the stuff you used to be able to pick up. Then you're yanking the cord to an electric lawn mower complaining that the Sox aren't on in the day no more."

"The golden years they call them," Joe said.

"I'm just running a business to pay my guys and I don't have two nickels for myself."

"It's the same for me, Tony."

"You don't have the overhead I do."

"I'm telling you, Tony, it's the same for me. I don't have a nickel. Would you like me any better if I could prove I didn't?"

Tony shrugged.

"You've been pretty creative lately about distancing yourself."

"I have a wife, and a kid on the way," Joe said. "I don't know what else to tell you."

Tony was staring at the floor. His eyelids were

65

starting to fall.

"Why don't you get married, Tony?"

"Last thing I need is a joint return."

Tony's head nodded.

"You want to sleep here?"

"No," Tony said while shaking his head. "May as well take me home."

"If you don't call Brian tomorrow and apologize, I'm going to send you a bill for my professional services rendered."

Gleason drove Tony home. "Give me a call tomorrow and we'll get your truck."

"Thanks, Joe."

At home Joe tossed his clothes into a ball and climbed back into bed.

"Everything all right?" Maria asked.

"Yeah, fine," Joe said. "I just found out everything's changing."

"I could've told you that."

"Yeah, but I wouldn't have listened."

"I could've told you that too," Maria said.

"We can move the poster of Cagney if you want."

"I'll just move the mirror. That way we can't see him looking down at us. It won't bother me if I can't see him all of the time."

"Fair enough," Joe said before tackling sleep.

FROM THE CLOCK radio former bass player for The Rolling Stones started to play the opening scale to "Under My Thumb."

Maria woke up, poked the doze button, and disturbed her husband.

"Did you sleep, last night?"

"A little. You?"

"A little. I think your father was up."

"He was. Twice. My mother twice and my grandfather once."

"I thought it was your father five times," Maria said.

"No, it was two, two, and one," Joe confirmed.

"How can you tell?"

"My father, gravity, my mother doesn't flush at night and my grandfather uses a pail and then just empties it in the toilet. It has that gulping sound."

Maria turned, cotton-candying most of the covers. "Christ," she said, "I'm in for a long haul."

"I could've told you that," Joe said.

TEN

SNOW WAS FALLING. The Big Man poured himself some herbal tea and looked out the window and through the fire escape. To his disappointment, he could tell there wouldn't be much to this snowfall since they were large flakes, but there was enough to accumulate on the wrought iron.

While yo-yoing his tea bag, he said to his beagle, "Someone's plucking geese. Big flakes, that means there won't be too much snow."

Sitting down with his tea in hand, he placed four bank-fresh one hundred dollar notes on a kitchen table made of American cherry. With a pair of scissors he trimmed an eighth of an inch off one side of each of the hundred dollar bills. He pulled out his wallet and slid in the bills. They now fit to his satisfaction inside the fold. Next, he doubled up a rubber band around the wallet to protect himself from pickpockets.

Two weeks had passed since his Harvard Yard meeting with Senator Custance. The Big Man had had things figured out long before he'd even met with the Senator but knew as a businessman not to make matters seem too easy. There was a risk factor and years of goodwill that clients had to pay for, and if the project comes together too quickly, clients are less likely to understand that. As a general rule, he made the simple jobs look tough and the tough jobs look simple.

He took out a pad and pencil and sketched what he had in mind. After finishing his tea, he put a doggy sweater on his beagle and took him for a walk along Commonwealth Avenue in Boston. He crossed over to New-bury Street via Dartmouth Street and met State Senator Richard J. Custance outside the Travis Caf .

"Don't hand it to me," the Big Man said. "Why don't you kneel down and pat my dog. Ask me questions about him."

Senator Custance did as instructed. The dog wagged his tail and held its head up to the snowflakes. Custance asked questions about the old beagle, and the Big Man answered quite amicably.

An inch of fluffy snow had dusted the sidewalk, but foot traffic and ice-melt products tossed out by the shop owners trampled much of it.

"Okay," the Big Man said, "drop it in the snow by the dog."

With impressive sleight of hand, the senator reached inside his Brooks Brothers topcoat and dropped a sack as if he was still patting the dog. The Big Man bent over and scooped up his dog, then nodded to the Senator and walked away. The Senator looked down at the side-walk. The sack was gone.

WITH THE WAY Dutch O'Brien was swimming in the chair in front of Joe Gleason's desk, Joe would have sworn his first murder case had just walked in through the door.

"What's up?" Gleason put to the prospective client.

Dutch ran a hand through a slick mop of jet-black hair.

"Well, ya know . . .I probably don't need a lawyer, but, like, I gotta find out if I can do something. Ya know, find out if it's okay and stuff."

"You can tell me anything, Dutch. It's privileged communication. I can't tell anybody without your say-so."

"Well, I don't want you to think I'm weird, but, like, I wanna marry my cousin."

Dutch did some more squirming after he got it out, and fat spilled into every crevice of the chair.

"Okay. What is she?" Gleason asked. "First cousin—second cousin?"

Dutch twisted his face and thought for a moment.

"Let me see if I can get this, and you can tell me. My mother's sister's kid is the girl I wanna marry."

"So it's your aunt's daughter. That would make her your first cousin."

"Yeah, but she's half Italian."

"Okay," Gleason conceded, "I can look into that, but it still may make her your first cousin. I can check the statute."

Gleason crossed his leg. There was a hole in the leather bottom of his wing tip about the size of a knot-hole.

"Good, this is starting to come together," Dutch said.

"Now, what's her name?"

"My aunt?"

"No, the woman you want to marry."

"Victoria."

"And how old is Victoria?"

"Fifteen."

"How old are you?"

"Thirty-nine and a half."

A pause.

"Okay. Are you two going out?"

"No. But, I, like, only see her a couple times a year, and they were over last weekend. We went to mass and she had this sweater on. Then when it comes time to go to communion, she takes the sweater off and just unleashes her fuckin' bombs." Dutch held his hands out from his chest to describe the size of her breasts. "I mean, the whole church is looking at her tits, and I'm walking behind her, and everybody thinks she's my girlfriend. I mean it felt good. But I just wanna marry her, ya know. I know it's weird, but can you do it?"

"Well, remember, Dutch, she is fifteen. Does she know about your feelings?"

"No. I figured I'd talk to you first."

"Are you working?"

"I'm gonna get a truck and start a landscaping business in the spring."

"Good. But to answer your question, it is possible to marry your first cousin in Massachusetts with a judge's approval."

"And where she's half Italian, I might be able to get that."

"I'll see just how that might play into things, Dutch, but what I was going to say is that she is only fifteen years old. My advice is to wait until she's eighteen and of a legal capacity to make her own decisions. I think we should focus on getting your business up and running, and in a few years' time, if she's willing to marry you, we could look into it then."

"Yeah, that might be good, because right now I'd have to pay you on contingency because I don't have any money."

"Contingency?"

"Right. Like, I'd invite you to the wedding because that would be like fifty bucks a plate and you can bring your wife so it would be double that."

"Fair enough, Dutch," Gleason said.

Joe leaned back in his chair after Dutch left and said to himself, "Joseph C. Gleason, Attorney at Law—'I WORK FOR FOOD.'"

ELEVEN

A FRY COOK at Benson's Diner in Wayland ran a forgotten Mass Millions ticket through a lottery scan and then shook his head at the plumber's helper. A van outside honked impatiently for the lottery hopeful. It was back to the pipes after lunch. The cook had a smile somewhere.

The cook removed the pencil from behind his ear and walked to the end of the counter. He wrote down orders on the inside panel of cigarette cartons. "What can I get you?" he asked the Big Man.

"I'll take two cheeseburgers—rare. They good size?" He cupped his hands together like they were the two halves of a bun to show what he meant about size.

"Yeah, they're a good size. About a quarter pound. We don't cook them rare. Medium's as rare as we go," the cook said. The Big Man seemed not to listen.

"They come with fries?"

The cook pointed to the menu with his pencil. "Chips," he answered.

"Can I get fries?"

The cook nodded and scribbled. "To drink?"

"If I get the fries, do I still get the chips?"

The cook nodded.

"But I still get two bags of chips since I got two burgers, right? I want only one order of fries."

"Right."

"Okay. Put the chips in a bag to go and I'll take milks with that. Two pints," the Big Man said. "And a straw when you get a chance. I'll take the milks before the meal if that's okay."

"Want a glass for the milks?"

The Big Man thought for a moment. He didn't see a dishwasher, just a sink.

"No. Just the straw."

The Big Man palmed his milks, moved over to the front window, and sat on a low, vinyl bench that had collected a few newspapers over breakfast. In front of him was a small, round table with a boomerang pattern. He thumbed through a *People Magazine* and learned who the sexiest people alive were. The picture window was to his back. He didn't like that. He kept looking out at the thin traffic moving up and down the Boston Post Road, which runs all the way to Oregon. A dark blue Oldsmobile sedan pulled in just as his lunch and bags of chips were delivered. Now he could eat.

The driver of the sedan looked to be in his late sixties and had thick gray hair parted to the side. He was wearing bifocals with thick black frames and brushed something off a gray cardigan Izod before hoisting the back of his tan Dickies.

Without getting up, the Big Man extended a hand and the driver of the sedan sat down. His face was red and oily. The Big Man handed him a piece of paper with a sketch on it, and then bit into his first cheeseburger.

The driver of the sedan adjusted his eyeglasses. He had a gin blossom nose, but even through his bifocals his eyes were lean and focused. He studied the sketch on the paper.

"Excellent," the driver of the sedan said.

The Big Man just chewed with his milk on deck in his left hand.

"When?" the driver of the sedan asked.

"After Christmas," the Big Man said, and then sucked on his straw.

"Excellent. I can do this. It will be lighter than you expect and fewer pieces too. Unless you want it more complicated."

"We like simple on this one."

The driver of the sedan fiddled with his eyeglasses again and released a toothy smile.

The Big Man handed his associate the bag of chips and said, "Lunch."

While paying for his meal, the Big Man purchased a two dollar scratch ticket and tucked it into the inside pocket of his blazer.

❖

In his Olds—somewhere along the Boston Post Road in Sudbury—the driver pulled his eyeglasses to the tip of his nose, looked into the bag of chips, and saw that the bag held his four thousand dollar deposit. He didn't bother to count the stack. The Big Man was always true to his word.

❖

FIVE YEARS AGO
THE GENERAL STORE
GREEN HARBOR, MASSACHUSETTS (THE IRISH RIVIERA)

Joe Gleason waited in line with a case of Miller High Life, four Styrofoam beer holders, and a Styrofoam cooler with two bags of ice in it.

The two young women in front of him had twenty-five bags of ice boxed and on the counter.

The young women began carting the ice out into their jeep while Gleason settled up. Outside he said to the one with the dark, baby oiled skin. "That's a lot of ice."

"Twenty-five bags." She adjusted the knot to her bikini top.

"At five pounds a bag that would be a hundred and twenty-five pounds."

"That would be right," the young woman said.

Her friend in the passenger's seat watched as the ice started to melt.

"Is there a party or something?"

A shrug.

"Or something."

"Where?"

"Down on the Horseshoe by the opening. All day and all night."

"Can I buy you a beer at the Gurnet Inn later?"

"I have a boyfriend."

"He can buy his own beer. I'm just a poor law student."

"We have to go. The ice is melting," the one from the passenger's seat said.

The young woman talking to Joe started backing out. "Swing by. Bring your friends."

Joe's hands suddenly grew sweaty. "What's your name?"

"Maria."

"Okay. I'll see you later." He fumbled at the mouth. "Okay well, en-enjoy your ice."

"HERE YOU GO," Tick said, while handing his boss, Jim O'Kane, a cup of coffee and swinging his large frame into the van.

"Thanks."

"Turn the radio off, I'm sick of it."

"You're a ball buster. You know that, Tick?" O'Kane turned off "All Night Long," by Joe Walsh.

"Yeah, I know it. Whatta ya think of that ass?"

"Not bad. A little pancaked, but not bad on her."

"Just bend it over—that'll round it out right," Tick said.

"That won't get rid of the sag, though."

"Who cares? Too much screwing's not good for you anyway."

"Why's that?" O'Kane asked.

"Turns you queer."

"Whatta ya mean?"

"Just that. Too many rides will turn a man queer, is all."

"You're winding me up."

"Are you worried, Jim?"

"Would the IRA give up alcohol, tobacco, and firearms for Lent? I just never heard that before. Where'd you hear that?"

"No place. Just makes sense, is all. You start plowing every broad you see, you start to grow bored, and then you feel the need to experiment. And what do you experiment with but other men. It only makes complete sense."

O'Kane was getting his Irish up. "So what about women?" His voice rose. "If they get laid too much, do they turn queer for other women?"

"No. My theory on women is that, even if they have sex with each other, they're not queer. You see— women don't like men to begin with. They like sex just as much as men and nobody wants to admit it," Tick said. "I mean, there's no way women could like men. We're all hairy and gross."

"Well, you just think we're gross because you're not gay. If you were a woman, you'd likely find men attractive."

"So you're after saying men can be attractive?"

"To women, yeah. Not me," O'Kane said. "Now let's drop this straight away before I pull the van over so we can discuss this outside."

"Don't be getting angry at me because you're found out to be gay."

O'Kane was red. "I said to stop it, Tick—straightaway. You're getting way too close to the bone now."

Tick rolled up his hand and put it to his lips like it was a megaphone and announced, "Mr. Jim O'Kane, this is Sean Glynn on Kerry's ninety-four and a half's Big Breakfast, and you've just been wound up by your friend Tick Dillon."

O'Kane banged his palm on the steering wheel and laughed.

"Oh, Jesus Christ, you fuck. You really wound me up good, Tick. Fair fucking play to ya. I was just about to pull the van over and have discussion."

They laughed for a while, then O'Kane asked, "Now, what's on for tonight?"

78

"I told Mick I'd meet him over his place for a beer. You're welcome to join us."

"Can't. I got some things. Don't get too pissed. I could use you tomorrow."

"So, when do you think I can get in as a partner, Jim? I've got to start making some real money. I think I've done my time on the cross."

"Let me talk to my accountant. It's near the end of the year, and it doesn't make sense for you to jump in now. For either of us. It might kill us both in taxes. You're better off filling out the easy form this year and we can get you in around the first of the year. We'll see how it goes. Maybe talk to Joe Gleason, too, and see if we should incorporate."

"Right," Tick said, "next year."

All part of the master plan.

MARY BOYLE WAS lying in bed looking out the window. Tick was late. In fact, he would never show up at all.

She saw two clouds drifting. They resembled two giant robins. The cloud on the left looked like the mother and the cloud on the right a hatchling. The mother's beak touched the beak of its young as if it were feeding it, but soon the clouds began to elongate and the beaks drifted apart so that the feeding became impossible. The hatchling seemed to transform into a hound and the mother robin into a duck.

Slowly, the clouds drifted behind the naked branches of a red oak and then out of the window's view completely. Somewhere, they dissolved into the late afternoon.

Night dropped. Mary watched the digital clock by her bedside pump the blood-red minutes. She felt her stomach and began to cry.

❖❖

TWELVE

THE FIRE HAD too many beer cans in it, and although the occupants didn't notice it—or maybe just didn't care—smoke was starting to fill up the garage.

Mick Hunt stuffed a birch log into the wood stove and, with the tip of his boot, closed one of the cast iron gates halfway.

"All right, cut the shit with all the beer cans," he said.

"The wood's fuckin' green," Tony Vaccaro said.

"It's you fuckin' light weights throwing away half your beers. Besides, I told you to put the empties aside for the Christmas party."

"You cheap fuck," Tick said. "I'm headed home for Christmas besides." He was sitting on a nested bundle of white oak flooring.

Tony Vaccaro's father, Sonny, was there watching the fire, his arms crossed. "How's your grandfather, Joe?" he asked.

"Still thinks the garden's the dump, but he's doing okay."

Mr. Vaccaro smiled and then looked at the fire some more. "What we used to do on Sundays in East Boston was build a big fire and cook lamb."

"Would you put it right on the fire?" Hunt asked.

"Oh, Christ no. Jesus. Just above the coals. There was no foil back then so we'd just put it right above the coals. But you know, everyone would get together because the houses were so close, and it was a meal, that's all it was. We were crowded. We all had little gardens. Get the garden as close as we could to the cesspool and we'd get these big tomatoes and peppers."

Hunt scowled and took a swig of beer to wash it down. "Were they any good?"

"Oh sure, the best I ever tasted. Now the goddamn place is Logan Airport."

"People lived on Logan Airport?" Tick asked.

Mr. Vaccaro didn't answer. He saw what was coming. "Jesus, I'll see ya fellas, too much beer in here now."

Bob Kerr walked into the garage carrying a case of Budweiser. His girlfriend, Maureen, carried a brown bag containing cigars. Joe Gleason got talked into one more beer and took a cigar for himself and handed another to Tony Vaccaro. Hunt refused.

"How's your grandmother?" Gleason asked Tony.

Tony turned his hands and said, "Hanging in there, anyway. I need to talk to you about her one of these days."

Bob Kerr saw an opening. "Hey'd you hear about that piker McDermott?"

Hunt said, "That guy McDermott's tighter than a frog's ass."

Joe Gleason laughed and then held his cigar into the flame of the wood stove until he got the tip of it half lit. Kerr tossed him a lighter to finish the job.

"Who's McDermott again?" Gleason asked while puffing.

"Contractor out of Brighton," Kerr said. "Guy took me out golfing when I started out. His socks were hanging around his ankles like they were Glad trash bags. Guy thought he was going to sucker me into banging nails

82

for experience, like he was doing me a favor letting me work for him or something."

"He always pulls that shit," Hunt said.

"So what the fuck happened to him?" Gleason said.

"I guess a couple weeks ago," Kerr said, "someone knocked the starch out of his skull. I guess it happened right in that alley up behind the Corrib. Then he crawls all the way to the Green Briar until someone gets him up to that hospital there. What is it again?"

"Saint Elizabeth's," Vaccaro said.

"Yeah," Kerr said, "he crawled all the way to Saint E's."

"Probably collecting change along the way, too," Hunt said.

"Probably," Kerr said. "He called me from Framingham once about something, and as a joke I told him I'd buy him lunch. The fuckin' guy burns up twenty bucks worth of gas and was back here before I could disconnect the phone. Then I ask him at lunch if he was in Nam, and he grunts something into his sandwich that he wanted me to think was a yes."

"Where'd you hear about the attack?" Gleason asked.

Kerr's girlfriend, Maureen, answered: "My friend works the door at the Briar, and he was telling me and Bob last night."

"Guy was always on the sauce—always," Hunt said.

"Strong as a bull too," said Kerr. "Guy could lift anything."

"It was cheap strength," said Hunt. "He was just

83

too cheap to hire a worker. So what happened to him after that?"

Tick Dillon finished his beer and lifted another out of the case Kerr had brought. He lit a cigarette and sat back down closer to the fire. He watched the flames dance; they were making him tired.

Kerr shrugged. "Haven't heard. I guess the guy's gonna be scrambled eggs, though, if he makes it, but I guess he's just plugged in, so chances aren't good."

Hunt shook his head. "Christ, if you can break that cheap Scot's Cro-Magnon squash, no one's safe. He wasn't married, was he?"

"Don't think so," Kerr said.
"Saw him—" Tick stopped himself and then realized it would be too awkward to change the course of what he had started to say. He looked directly at the fire as he spoke. "I saw him a few weeks ago with a girl. I don't know if anything came of it."

"Where was that?" Hunt asked.

"The Village."

Gleason looked at Tick.

Hunt shook his head. "He was a cheap fuck."

"I won't go to his wake," Kerr said.

Gleason looked down and saw Tick peel the label off of his beer, then ball it up and whip it into the flames. The birch log that Hunt had thrown in was starting to pop.

JIM O'KANE was too hung over to man the wheel, so Tick Dillon was making the cuts down Felton Street in Waltham on their way to McCallen's, the hardwood-flooring supplier.

"Change the station," O'Kane said.

"You don't like the Pretenders?" Tick said.

"I don't always like female vocalists because then I can't imagine I'm the one singing."

They drove some more and Tick elevated the level of their discussion. "I don't know, Jim. Do you suppose a meteor really could hit the world and wreck it?"

"Absolutely, Tick. It doesn't even have to hit the earth. If it's big enough, all's it has to do is hit the ocean and there'll be massive floods everywhere."

Tick drew his lips together and shook his head.

"Jesus Christ all mighty."

"Goddamn right," Jim said. "So what's up for lunch, meat or fish?"

"I could go for a fish and chip."

"Good call. McDonald's or Burger King?"

THIRTEEN

"Is Evel Knievel coming here?" Tony Vaccaro said to the high school dropout who was on his knees trying to lay a herring bone pattern with bricks.

"What?" the kid answered. He had no idea what Vaccaro was talking about, nor did he know who Evel Knievel was.

"I said, is Evel Fuckin' Knievel gonna come here?"

"What!"

"Don't mouth off. The fuckin' walkway. Will you get up and look at your work? It's a fuckin' ramp. Evel Knievel could jump Snake Canyon using this thing as a ramp. I leave here for an hour and you butcher the fuckin' thing. Pull up the last ten courses and start over. Get up and look at it first. I told you to get up every couple courses and look."

Joe Gleason caught the upbraiding and laughed. "Tony. Talk to you for a minute?"

"Joe, what's up? Christ, my father would've kicked the ever-living shit outta me if I ever did shit work like that fuckin' kid. Christ, help sucks these days."

"Yeah, well, we're all becoming our old men, I think. Kid seems like a good worker. Don't be so tough on him."

"He's okay. I just gotta put him through it, ya know?"

"And some day he'll thank you for it. That it?"

"Either that or fire me," Vaccaro said. "So, what's up?"

"Listen, you know if O'Kane ever did work for that

guy McDermott?"

"He did. I don't know about recent, but he did. Why?"

Gleason shook his head. "Nothing. It's stupid."

Vaccaro didn't have a degree, but he could see the distance. "If McDermott owed him money, I wouldn't put it past 'im."

"What do you mean?"

"What do I mean? I mean, if McDermott owed O'Kane money, I wouldn't put it past 'im. You know exactly what I mean. I'd do the same, only I'd have it done. You have to get paid." Vaccaro didn't look so uneducated now.

"Yeah," Gleason said, "gotta get paid."

Vaccaro looked away from Gleason and swallowed before he said, "Joe, I gotta ask you a favor."

"Go ahead."

"My grandmother's not doing too well." Vaccaro found something to look at. "She's up the nursing home and she keeps asking for a lawyer."

"Yeah, whatever you need, Tony."

"I don't know if she's all there anymore, but she just keeps talking. Ya know what I'm saying?"

"No problem, Tony. I'll talk to her. I know what you're saying."

Gleason and Vaccaro watched for a moment as the high school dropout shaved off a layer of stone dust with a square shovel and then started the courses of bricks all over again.

Laying bricks would be a long life, the kid thought. He could start his own business and have weekends off and any other days he wanted too.

"Yeah, it's a nice place," Joe Gleason said to his younger sister Jessica after getting the furnished tour of her new home in Norwood. "You may want to get rid of the extra toothbrush in the bathroom before ma and dad visit, though."

They went out to the kitchen. It was understood in the Gleason family that the kitchen was where you discussed matters. Joe looked at the refrigerator and saw that it was covered with fruit stickers.

"Remember we used to fight over who got the banana stickers?" Joe asked.

Jessica lifted her right bang behind her ear and said with her arms folded, "How do you stand it at home, Joe?"

"I just deal with it. I don't mind it, really; we have our own space."

"What about Maria?"

"It gets to her sometimes, but she understands. I never thought my little sister would be raking in three times what I am. I should've charged you for that closing."

"Not too late."

"Forget it. I'm in so deep it wouldn't help anyway. But, when I'm a millionaire and start buying and trading stocks, just forgo the commission for me, okay?"

Jessica looked into his eyes. There was silence for a moment. She broke it.

"What's wrong, big brother?"

"Nothing. I guess I'm just a little tired. So, we ever gonna hear about the guy who brushes his teeth here?"

"His name's Mark."

"Is he Catholic?"

"Does it matter?"

"Makes it easier."

"Why?"

Joe Gleason smiled. "At least tell me he has a good job."

"He's a prosecutor here in Norfolk County," Jessica said.

"Where's he from?"

"Wellesley."

"Wellesley! Another member of the landed gentry putting poor folks behind bars. Sounds to me like the product of parental ambition."

"A little judgmental, aren't we? You don't even know him."

"That's my point. He's mixing it up with my sister, and we've never even met him. Why not?"

"Because. It's not like my family is some kind of success story. I love mom and dad, but I'm moving on, Joe, and you can't handle it. I'm not a kid. You were married a year at my age. You refuse to get ahead or be a success."

"I refuse to compromise. I believe in the values my parents taught me, and I'm not ashamed of where I came from. I don't need to move away or hide from who I am."

"Does Maria feel that way? Have you asked her? Does she want to live with her in-laws forever?"

Joe Gleason stopped talking. He shook his head and started up again. "I don't know. I'm just tired. I'm sorry. Maybe I'm wrong about everything. But I can be judgmental about who's sleeping with my sister."

"He's a good guy, Joe."

"Good. Listen, I gotta get a drink."

"Do you want me to come with you?"

"No. I'll just go alone, I think."

Jessica gave him a hug and began to cry. "I think you're alone too much, Joe."

"Things will change when the baby comes. I want a baby girl. Everybody thinks Irishmen want sons, but it's not always true."

He tightened his lips and left before his baby sister saw his tears. A drink was what he needed.

THE HISTORICAL MAN.

An Irishman wearing his Sunday finery at The Shamrock in Norwood said he'd have another. He was seventy-three and had mitts that could palm a Black Angus.

"My plan," Joe said, "is to get enough money and move over to Ireland. My grandfather was born in Ireland and still has family in Kerry though his brother Michael boozed a good portion of the farm away. When I earn enough money, I'll take my wife and daughter over and we'll start a bed and breakfast." Joe swallowed some beer. "I don't know why my grandfather ever came to this place."

"If he didn't, you wouldn't be around to dislike it," the Irishman said. "Americans complain about what they don't have because they've never been without anything."

Joe smiled into his beer. "Well, this is only temporary. My first step is to find some time to apply for dual citizenship. I wish I had a trade, but I was pushed into law. I want to see the fruits of my labor. You don't always get that working law."

"Sometimes there's nothing more permanent than temporary," the Irishman said before getting up to visit the loo. When he returned, a bottle of beer was waiting for him.

"Oh," he said, "I wasn't going to have another bottle of beer, but now that you've bought it, I can't let it go to waste."

"So what's a bullock anyway?" Joe Gleason asked.

"It's a bull that's been castrated."

The definition triggered the male "ouch" look.

"How many do you have, a couple of hundred?"

"Oh, no. I have only thirty-seven acres, and it takes about two acres to feed each one. I keep only about ten."

"Two acres? Guess I'll need more land."

The Irishman pulled out a black pipe and some plug tobacco.

"Well, it depends on the land, you see. Some of it's salt marsh and too hilly—stony. In some areas they can feed on as little as an acre. In the spring I can keep them on an acre, but you see, you have to have enough hay to keep them in the winter. Keep them fed and keep them warm."

"So you have to collect the hay for the winter months."

"Yes, that's right, yes, Joe," the Irishman answered. With a small jack-knife, he was shaving off bits of tobacco from the plug and packing them into the bowl of his Peterson pipe. The right side of his pipe bowl had a dip in it from being lit so often.

"How much do you get for one cow?"

91

"A couple of years ago, you could get seven hundred pounds, but now it's down to as little as five hundred pounds."

"Why is that?"

"Well, the economy in Russia has gone down and the demand isn't as much."

The old gent put a wooden matchstick to the pipe and got it going.

Gleason paused to take in the pipe's aroma before asking, "How much does a butcher make on, say, one bullock?"

The Irishman pulled on his pipe and then pointed the mouthpiece at Gleason. Leaning over his pipe, he confided, "Well, somewhere someone's getting a colossal handful because, by the time a butcher sells it, it's worth twenty-two hundred pounds, and no one knows how it gets that high."

"They must use everything."

"They use everything but the 'moo,' as we say."

They had one more as they discussed the new Euro Dollar. It would be a long time before England bought into it, the Irishman confided over a few more beers and a fresh bowl of tobacco. "A long time," he held. "But the economy will eventually move it in that direction."

An ocean away from Ireland, the grass is always greener.

FOURTEEN

TICK AND JIM O'Kane were finishing up a round at the Irish Village.

"I'm telling you, Tick, if an Irishman is a laborer he's generally termed simple, but any other ethnic group that labors is termed oppressed."

"A man can't care what others think," Tick said. "Work is a gift from God, not a punishment. And if you care about your work, you care about yourself. The others don't matter none. It's true. You are what you think you are."

They were next to a couple of stiffs enrolled as barflies who spent most of their time complaining about how affirmative action kept them off the force. They had enough in them to decide on mixing it up with a couple of Paddys.

"Fuckin' Aer Lingus carpenters," the stiff with the better English said as Tick and O'Kane were walking by them.

In the trades it is contended that when the Irish immigrate to America via Aer Lingus Airways, they determine what their trade is going to be on the flight over. Thus, an Aer Lingus carpenter has become nomenclature to describe a hack, or inexperienced Irish tradesman.

Tick planned to keep going, but the comment put O'Kane's Irish into full gear. "What was that you say?"

"Ya heard 'im, ya smelly Mick flounder-belly," came out from the second stiff.

"I did hear," O'Kane said, "but what I can't believe is that you said that to my friend here. Perhaps you'd like

93

to step outside like gentlemen and discuss it proper?"

"Let's make it quick," better English said.

As the two stiffs began to climb down off their stools, Tick and O'Kane caught them off balance by kicking the stool legs out from under them. The detractors started to wobble and Tick banged their heads together, and by that time, O'Kane was ready to step in and give them both a few shots to the ribs with the toe of his boot. When the stiffs were on the floor, O'Kane picked up a stool and was about to clock them both when Tick grabbed it and said they had had enough. He had seen what O'Kane was capable of when he went to work on McDermott.

O'Kane threw the stool across the bar, broke away from Tick's grip and punched the door before walking out of the bar.

"Sorry, Liam," Tick said to the bartender.

Liam shook his head. "God have mercy, Tick. Your man has to get laid soon."

THE LITER OF Johnnie Walker Red huddling next to the Big Man was unopened, but it was his second bottle. The radio was maxed, and by the time the Big Man had found Massachusetts Avenue in East Lexington Susan Tedeschi was singing about it hurting so bad. He was sticking to Mass Ave since he knew following it would at least dump him off in Cambridge by Frank's Steakhouse and if he wanted to push it, he could follow it all the way into Boston. The same route Paul Revere traveled after quaffing a few tinkers of ale.

It was three-thirty in the morning, and his eyes were drawn heavily to the spears of light thrusting out from the street lamps and jousting the front hood of the car. The Buick he was trying to manipulate hit a bend just past the Follen Church, and the double yellow lines started to loop around to the left. The Buick followed them and so did an oncoming Dodge pickup truck. Then it was two pickups in the Big Man's eyes. He jammed on the brakes and somehow managed a j-turn. He doubled back about fifty yards and swung into a back entrance into Wilson Farm.

After he punched the gas pedal, the sandstone driveway began to spit out behind him as the Buick aimed itself directly at a greenhouse.

His seat belt was on when the Buick smashed through the greenhouse the migrant farm workers from El Salvador had named El Bud because that's where they drank beer in conclave during the winter months.

The air bag punched him in the face and popped open his nose. With manic force, he kept trying to rake it away before it deflated, all the while hitting the gas pedal and playing the steering wheel back and forth. Two poinsettia tables crashed to their demise. A clay pot exploded against the Big Man's windshield like an egg whipped against a stone wall, and his tires crunched and sprayed the three quarter-inch limestone floor of El Bud.

Limestone riddled the sheets of greenhouse glass, fracturing them into sword-like pieces.

He fired the automatic shift into reverse, and the rear end of the Buick shot out of the greenhouse. He followed a tractor's path to the farm after managing to get the car into drive.

The front end of the Buick was pounding up and down on the ground and throwing the Big Man's head into the frame of the windshield. He gripped the steering wheel with such force that it started to bend.

With his left hand, he hit a button he thought opened the front passenger's window, but in fact it opened the rear passenger's window. He grabbed the Johnnie Walker by the throat and tomahawked it into the passenger window. The bottle shattered, and the smell of hard booze permeated the cabin of the car.

By the time he hit forty, blood—chilled by the rush of cold air coming in through the rear passenger's window—was rolling down his face like fresh beet juice. By the time he hit sixty, the car buckled in the muddy furrows.

He gave the column shift a series of upper cuts and clobbered the gas pedal, trying to rock himself free, but only further compromised his position. After a few unsuccessful attempts, he got the idea that he was spending the night in Lexington. He killed the engine and removed the keys from the ignition shaft. He reached for his bottle and halfway there remembered his foolishness. He passed out after his head thumped forward and butted the steering wheel. With his forehead resting on the steering wheel, his lower lip—half bitten off—ran a plumb line of blood down to the driver's floor mat.

Less than two minutes later, Street Sergeant Susan Jacobs of the Lexington Police Department was there, processing the scene. She flashed a light on the Big Man and saw that what wasn't red on his face was blue. She removed the seat belt strap that had gotten wrapped around the Big Man's neck. Had she not done so, the weight of his head would have strangled him to death.

❖

EIGHTEEN MONTHS EARLIER, detective Jack Mundi had been told by his doctor that his glands were swollen and that they should take a biopsy just as a precaution. Mundi had just looked at his watch when he heard the news. Six months later, his red blood cells were taking what seemed to be an irreversible nosedive. His blood had become too poisoned, and while the Big Man was masticating cheeseburgers at Benson's, Mundi was given three months to live. He still looked at his watch.

Presently, Detective Reva Smith rested half of her behind on Mundi's desk. Her blue wrap skirt tightened around her muscular thigh. "Wanna hear something funny?" she asked.

Mundi leaned. "Yeah, I could use a funny," he said. His eyes followed her stockings. It was all she wore underneath her wrap skirt. With a little manipulation of his swivel Mundi was able to complete the inspection.

"The Big Man tried to plow a farm in Lexington with his Buick Century last night."

"Drunk?"

"Very."

"It's like clockwork," Mundi said. "Every three years he falls off and goes out on a tear."

"What'd he do last time?"

"It was that McDonald's by the IHOP in Brighton. You know, near Parsons Street?" Smith didn't but nodded anyway. "He walks in there about ten-thirty at night after a four-day binge and orders a Whopper, or Big Mac is it? Whatever the Christ they have, and tells the guy no onions. Well, the guy's a Haitian and doesn't speak English too well, but takes the order with initiative, and when the big guy bites into his—" Mundi lost his thought.

97

Smith filled him in. "Big Mac."

"Yeah, Big Mac—Whopper, whatever the fuck it was—the thing had onions, so the Big Man goes back in, walks around the counter, punches the guy out, and sticks his hand in the fry oil until there was nothing left but bone."

"Doesn't sound like the type of person who would settle on just the white of the egg."

"Not a chance. He'll need a little more than Saint John's Wart to smooth out the lines."

"So'd the Big Man get prosecuted?" Smith asked.

"Never made it past pretrial conference. The only witness was the guy who got his hand fried, and then it was believed that this attorney, Lawrence Kennedy, had a few goons pay him a house call that put the fear of Papa Doc back in him. So now he's out tearing up Lexington."

"Yeah. I thought you said he never drove?"

"He doesn't—usually. He always takes the T or walks. Lexington's way out for him. I wonder why he was way out there. It'll be interesting to see whose car he had."

Smith said, "Maybe he went out to pick up his Thanksgiving turkey."

"Possibly, Detective. Who covers Lexington? Is it still Concord?"

"Yeah. Wanna jump on our bikes and head out there for the arraignment?"

Mundi looked over Smith's legs. She noticed and tilted her head to let her long auburn hair fall to the side. "Give me a few moments," he said. "I can't get up just yet." Mundi was dying but still functional.

Smith smiled and headed off for the women's room.

Mundi spoke up. "Hey, Smith."

"What?" she said.

"I told you I'm dying, didn't I?"

She made a thoughtful look and shrugged her shoulders. "I think I heard something about it, but you know how it is—you get caught up in things." She pretended to cover a yawn.

"Okay," Mundi said. "You need me to fetch a coffee?"

"Yeah."

"How do you take it?"

"Light—very light with one sugar," Smith said.

"Milk or cream?"

"Milk."

"Skim?"

"Fat milk."

"So real sugar then?" Mundi asked.

Smith gritted her teeth. "Make it straight up or draped over the saddle, for Christ's sake."

Mundi smiled. Had he known Smith was an Eastwood fan he might have taken care of that cancer earlier. He leaned with his hands behind his head. "The Big Man is up to something," he said to himself. "Doing what you love . . . Not a bad way to go out."

IN THE LADIES' room Smith washed her face with cold water then looked at herself in the mirror and figured she could hide her drinking for another year or so. She washed her hands next. The faucet was one of those automatic kinds that shut off before you've had a chance to wash all the soap from your hands. It took a few rounds before washing it all away.

FIFTEEN

A CUSTODIAN IN his early twenties, with sideburns that Derek Sanderson might envy, steered a heap of trash down the linoleum hallway of The Brick Village Nursing Home with a dry mop. His destination was a lime-green trash barrel tucked into a corner next to a fire extinguisher. After removing the barrel, the custodian directed his sweepings into the corner, leaned the dry mop against the wall, and put the barrel back.

"Nice," Joe Gleason said.

"Get to it latter," the custodian said.

There was an old lady sitting by the time clock with horn-rimmed glasses and slits along the toes of her Converse sneakers that were there to let her feet breathe pursuant to the orders of the visiting podiatrist.

"Honey," she said to Gleason, "is Peter coming today?"

Her brother Peter was a Quincy cop who'd been cold in the grave for better than fifteen years. He was also an alcoholic and used to show up just to eat his sister's lunch.

"I haven't heard, ma'am."

"He's going to be a priest."

"Well, that's good," Gleason said.

"Oh, to hell with you. You're a rotten egg anyway," she said and then stuck her tongue out at him. "You're for the birds."

Gleason turned to the nurse's station.

"I'm looking for a patient named Mrs. Sacco."

The nurse broke away from something titled the

"Bowel Book" and pointed with his pen. "They're residents—not patients. West 23."

Gleason walked down the hall, and a lady in a wheelchair with purple beads around her neck stopped him.

"Play cards with me, handsome?" She reached into her bosom and produced a pack.

"I can't right now. I'm visiting a friend."

"All right." She dropped her head into the flat of her hand and began sulking.

In West 23, Gleason found Mrs. Sacco upright in bed. The plastic coated mattress on the bed next to her had been wiped down with Lysol.

He could hear, in the background, an old man tied to his wheelchair shouting for whoever would listen, "Cut the ribbon! Cut the ribbon! Oh, God, cut the ribbon!" Joe shut the door to West 23 and with that, muffled the old man's plea.

"Mrs. Sacco . . . Joe Gleason."

She pulled her hands away from a pillow she was crocheting and said, "Joe Gleas."

She never pronounced the last syllable of people's surnames.

He leaned over her and took a kiss.

Mrs. Sacco wrapped her hands around his biceps. When Gleason was free, he opened the door to the common washroom, ran some cold water into a wax-coated cup, and held it for Mrs. Sacco to drink with his hand under her chin.

"Tony sent me up. He said you wanted a lawyer."

"You're a lawyer?" She held her hand to show that she had known him when he was just a kid. She also knew

102

him when he and Tony were testing out swear words and she overheard them. Gleason sweated that one out for a month, but old lady Sacco never told on them.

They talked for a bit, and then Joe said, "So, Tony told me you wanted a lawyer."

She squeezed her lips together and then said, "This is no good. I'm gonna save all my pills and tak'em at once."

"Why?"

She shook her head. "This is no good. I want if I get sick. . .No more. Just let me go."

"So if you get real sick, you don't want a bunch of doctors in here. Tony's no angel, but he's worried about the Church."

She made wingovers with her arms. "I just want to go."

"It's called a health proxy. You'll have to get a family member or someone who'll carry out your wishes when the time comes. And then the doctor has to agree. You understand what I'm saying?"

She shrugged. "I know . . .. You're a lawyer. You do it for me. That's what I want."

Gleason knew that Tony Vaccaro had sent him up there to talk his grandmother out of a health proxy, but the fact was she was lucid and capable of making her own decisions. She was his client, not the Vaccaros.

He searched for a compromise. He needed more time.

"What are you making?" Gleason asked.

"Ehh. Just a pillow."

"Listen. I'll look into what you want, and in the meantime, you make me a pillow. You know, it may take some time to research, but I'll keep you posted, okay? And don't save your pills from the nurse."

"I'll make you a pillow."

"Okay. I'll send Tony up with some more yarn."

He kissed her good-bye, and on the way back down the hall the woman in the purple beads once again removed an abridged deck of cards from her bosom and proposed a game of cards.

"That doesn't look like a full deck," Joe said.

The woman with the purple beads widened her eyes and craned her neck toward him to confide. "The brown skins come in at night and steal them. They stole three packs." She let him know what she meant with three fingers held up as she said it.

"I'm sorry to hear that," Joe said. "Can we play cards some other time?"

"Okay, Honey," she said and then put the cards back into her bosom.

At the nurse's station Joe stopped and asked the nurse, "How do you guys administer medicine around here?"

"We crush it up and mix it with apple sauce."

"For all the residents?"

"As long as I've been here. Otherwise they might pretend to swallow it and save up the pills and OD."

The old woman sitting next to the time clock said to Joe, "Honey, is Peter coming?"

Gleason looked at her and said, "Soon, ma'am . . .Soon."

"Okay, honey. You're a good egg. He's coming to collect me."

The custodian hadn't gotten around to the trash he had left in the corner, and Gleason didn't have the heart to tell the woman by the time clock that she was a resident.

BACK AT HIS office, Gleason called Tony Vaccaro.

"Tony, I talked with your grandmother."

"How'd it go?" Vaccaro asked.

"We'll see. I got her to drink some water. When are you going to see her next?" Gleason was peeling an orange.

"Today," Vaccaro said.

"Good. Bring her some yarn and some foam. The kind they stuff pillows with."

"Why?"

"Because she's making me a pillow. Get it up there today."

"Okay, Brudda."

Gleason threw the orange peelings in the wastebasket. Fruit sticker and all. A blue one.

❖ ❖

SIXTEEN

ANTHONY GLEASON OFFERED his son the morning newspaper and then spooned a chunk of oatmeal submerged in light cream.

"No thanks, Dad," Joe said.

"Don't you want to read it?"

"I do, it's just that I have a lot on my mind."

"Like what?" his father asked.

"Just stuff."

"Stuff your old man wouldn't understand, huh?"

"Just not that much energy to talk right now."

His father turned a hand to him and made an indifferent face. Gleason watched as his father pumped more Vermont maple syrup into his bowl of oatmeal.

"I guess," Joe said, "I just feel like I'm wasting my time on small matters that don't mean much. I thought I'd be doing more. And now I think something big's going on and I'm not sure what to do."

"You know," Anthony Gleason started, "there was this fellow in Prague who started a petition for peace just before all hell broke out in World War I. You know how many signatures the guy got on the petition?"

Joe made signs with his hands and face that he didn't.

"He got three. Three signatures. Three people who had the guts to stand up for peace. Do you know who the guy was who started that petition?"

"No," Joe said.

"It was Albert Einstein."

"So, what are you saying?"

"I'm saying that if more people had had the guts to sign that petition, Albert Einstein might have been just a footnote in history."

Gleason took the morning newspaper.

MARIA GLEASON FINISHED her first period class and walked into the teacher's room at Bedford High School. The only other person in the room was a paunchy, red-headed fellow in his early twenties who was trying to figure out how to buy himself a coffee.

"Need some help?" Maria asked.

"Yeah. I already bought two cans of juice from the machine over there just so I could have a couple of quarters for this thing, and now I haven't a clue."

MEANWHILE, JOE GLEASON was walking down the corridor on the way to visit his wife. He bumped into a former teacher.

"Mr. Wills," Joe said.

"Yes?" Mr. Wills answered not recognizing Joe.

"Are you teaching here now?"

"I transferred from Arlington High seven years ago. Were you one of mine?" He extended a hand.

"Yeah. Joe Gleason."

"Joe Gleason! How's prison?"

"I'm an attorney now."

"Are you on a diet?"

Mr. Wills walked away in a bray of laughter and Joe headed off to the teacher's room.

"HERE'S A DIME," Maria said. "It's only thirty-five cents, and it won't give you change. Just drop the change in the slot, but keep your finger pressed on that black button. If you take it off, it'll stop."

"Thanks. I'm Craig Winter, by the way."

"Maria Gleason. Who else are you today?"

"I'm subbing for Earth Science. I forget her name."

"You know, they have pastries down in the copy room by the office and a Mr. Coffee. And if you actually feel like paying, there's a change container."

"No buttons to deal with?" Winter asked.

"None."

Joe Gleason walked into the room and gave Maria a kiss on the cheek.

"What do you mean if you feel like paying?" Gleason said. "Don't tell me teachers steal!"

"Of course not," Maria said. "We're all saints. Even if some of us do listen to rock and roll."

"I listen in private," Winter said. "I still feel rebellious listening to the Beatles when my parents are around."

She introduced her husband to Winter and he looked disappointed. Up until then Winter had taken Maria's small talk for something more than what it was. All at once he noticed her ring and her pregnancy.

IT WAS A classic New England autumn morning. The sky was a clear blue, and the leaves were brilliant red, orange, and yellow neon; at their peak in the wake of death.

Joe and Maria decided to walk down The Great Road to the Olde Bedford Country Store—Established 1979—for a coffee. The wooden bench out front was cold, but they warmed it up quickly.

"So, what's with the visit? Things can't be so slow at the office that you can up and take off for the morning."

"I'll just tell people I was in court. I needed to get out and talk to you."

"What's wrong?"

"Maybe nothing, but remember I told you Tick came down talking about a collection case?"

"Yeah, and you didn't take it, I thought."

"I didn't, but that night a contractor in Brighton was beaten up near the Corrib. I just read in the paper that he died last night from the injuries."

"And you think Tick beat him up?"

"It's just weird. Bob Kerr was telling us about it the other night down at Hunt's garage, and I didn't think anything strange about it at the time, but Tick kind of fumbled when he was asked about the guy. And then it happened the night Tick spoke to me about the debt."

"That can be a tough area, Joe. I wouldn't go hanging Tick if I were you. Not to mention he's a client of yours and you shouldn't be talking about it."

"I know, but when I read in the paper today that this guy—his name's McDermott, by the way—was last seen at The Village, I'm thinking, Christ, the evidence keeps coming in. Then I've just got this feeling it was him."

"Ask him," Maria said.

"I thought of that, but then there's part of me that just doesn't want to know, and how could I ask a friend if he killed somebody? I mean, I just can't believe it. I don't even know if I do have a duty to keep quiet. He came in

109

and asked about a collection case and then he said some things down at Hunt's garage. That had nothing to do with me being an attorney."

"But didn't you tell me it's the client's perception of whether you're representing them? Your reasoning flows—at least in part—from your conversation with him in your office. Is there another attorney you can talk to?"

"I think I might head into Cutter and Dudley and talk to Lawrence Kennedy. I'd like to get into Boston anyway. You know, the strange thing is, if I did find out, I don't think I'd dime him out anyway."

"So why do you need to know?" Maria asked.

Before answering Joe shook his head and watched a dry oak leave spider across the street in the wind.

"That's one I can't figure," he said.

TICK DILLON AND Jim O'Kane were traveling down Sandy Pond Road in Lincoln. U2's "Bloody Sunday" came over the radio, and Tick retrieved two paint stirrers off the floor of the van and began using them against the dashboard as drumsticks. He and Jim were singing along with Bono at the top of their lungs. The encore was "Back in the Saddle" by Boston's bad boys, Aerosmith.

When the duet was over, Jim O'Kane turned off the radio and picked up a flathead screwdriver and spoke into the handle as if it were a microphone.

"That was absolutely fantastic, Tick."

"Thank you, Jim. Although I have to give my friends down at Woodhaven Paints a special thank you for furnishing me with these perfectly crafted paint stirrers. Brilliant percussion, really."

"They are brilliant, Tick. I noticed you prefer the

110

virgin wood as opposed to some of the newcomers in the field who use heavily painted stirrers."

"That's true, Jim. I don't mean to put the newcomers down, but I prefer the virgin for better all around feel and acoustic performance. The smoothness in the virgin line is unparalleled."

"I imagine the newcomers find it tough to penetrate, do they?"

"You could be on to something, Jim."

"Now, how long have you been playing the paint stirrers?"

"Since the womb really, Jim. I come from a long line of paint stirring genius stock."

"So what do you think of Boston, Tick?"

"I can say with unqualified certainty, Jim, that Boston is perhaps one of my favorite big venue towns along the Eastern seaboard here in the states."

"Now that certainly sounds unqualified. Will Boston be seeing you again soon, Tick?"

"I'll be in San Fran for a few engagements and then off to Texas, but if time permits, I'd love to get back to Bean Town."

"There you have it folks," Jim said, signing off. "That was Tick Dillon along with his now famous band, The Tongue and Grooves."

"Cheers, folks. God bless," Tick said.

SEVENTEEN

TRIAL COURT OF THE COMMONWEALTH
DISTRICT COURT DEPARTMENT, CONCORD
DIVISION
CONCORD, MASSACHUSETTS

THE METAL DETECTOR at the Concord District Courthouse was still unused and still in its packing wrap next to the front door. Mundi took a left into the lobby and walked in the door that read "Prosecutors Only." Reva Smith followed.

A DEFENSE ATTORNEY on the wooden bench outside the Prosecutor's room was nodding to a client as if he had the facts down from day one.

"It took him four hundred yards to pull me over," the client said. "Four hundred yards and then he pulls me over."

"Okay," the defense attorney said.

"That's four football fields and then he pulls me over. They can't do that."

"Okay," the defense attorney said.

MUNDI TURNED THE doorknob, leaned into the prosecutors' room with his hand still on the knob, and cut off a thin woman in a brown suit who had had a nose job and who was wearing a set of reading glasses she really didn't need. Just trendy. Her eighty-five dollar haircut was styled to look like it just fell into place.

"Who's got the Big Man?" he asked.

Nose Job held up the official police report after rifling a stack of files. "I do. And you are?"

"Detective Jack Mundi, and this behind me is Detective Reva Smith—Boston."

Smith pinched his behind before working her way against the doorjamb. Her breasts were parked against Mundi's right shoulder. He was learning to control himself, but still buttoned his overcoat in case there was a sudden change in shift.

"What's your connection to this?" Nose Job asked. "It was Lexington, right?"

"Yeah; just observation and theory, counselor. What session are you in?"

"One; down the hall, across from the clerk's office. They'll make an announcement, but you'll never hear it."

"Who was the arresting officer?"

Nose Job looked through the file. "Susan Jacobs. Sergeant Jacobs, L-P-D. I guess the guy's a mess, so it may be heard second call, but then again, maybe not. We have a quick judge today."

"Thanks, counselor."

Mundi walked in the opposite direction to get a drink from the fountain. He threw down some pills and drank. When he came up he said, "This'll be a six-month CWOF."

"CWOF," Smith said. "Isn't that something you put coffee in to keep it warm?

"It's Continued Without A Finding." Smith tried to look as if she'd been educated. "The Big Man refrains from being naughty for six months, and the charges are dropped."

"You know everything."

"What we need to do is talk to the cops. See what the hell the Big Man had on him when he was picked up. That might tell us something."

"What do you mean? I thought we came out here just to hack around. We're not working this thing. Besides, we don't even know if there's anything to work. The guy was busted for OUI."

"I'm dying, I can do whatever I want. Besides, look who just walked in," Mundi tossed his jaw at a tall, lean man with curly white hair and manicured fingernails.

"Who's that?"

"The Grand Inquisitor himself: Lawrence Kennedy of Cutter and Dudley. You don't see him in district court. He's up at Superior with all the capital crime bullshit. Dollars to doughnuts he belongs to our guy. The Big Man's making sure he doesn't find himself in Billerica."

"Can you CWOF an OUI?"

"Mine was," Mundi said.

Smith looked around and saw the prosecutors and defense attorneys conducting pretrial conference in the hallway and said, "What a way to run the railroad."

"This is it," Mundi said.

TRIAL COURT OF THE COMMONWEALTH DISTRICT COURT DEPARTMENT, CONCORD DIVISION
CONCORD, MASSACHUSETTS

THE CLIENT WITH the football field argument was walking out of the courthouse with his attorney.

"You should have told him," the client said, "it took him four hundred yards to pull me over; that's four football fields to pull me over, for Christ's sake."

"Okay," the defense attorney said after clearing his car alarm with his right hand still in his trench coat pocket.

He was out of court early that morning.

It was a quick judge.

EIGHTEEN

STANDING ON THE Battle Green in Lexington center, just ninety minutes after the Big Man pleaded not guilty at his arraignment, Detective Reva Smith found herself putting together the following words and saying them to Detective Mundi:

"You don't have to tell me. I fuckin' know. Just society in general."

❖

"That's a cute dog," Smith said. "What is that?"

Mundi blew on his coffee. "Mutt, it looks like. Maybe a lab-greyhound mix."

"I love dogs more than people."

"Yeah, me too. You don't see as many mutts around anymore. I wonder why?"

"Because of all the yuppies."

"What do the yuppies have to do with it?" Mundi asked.

"Because they all want to have these perfect bred dogs, so they go out and find full breeds. They don't give a shit about mutts. It's a known fact."

"Jesus. I didn't know that."

"About five years ago," Smith said, "I was up New Hampshire camping, and my friend's aunt bred dogs - beautiful labs, too. Anyway, we saw the mother lab give birth. Then after, the lady was telling us about the last litter that these yuppies went on and on about, how they wanted to know the lineage of the dog they bought. They needed papers and kindred charts, for Christ's sake . . ."

Smith was cut off by a Lexington police officer.

116

"Folks, come on, you can't drink coffee on the Green. No food or drink on the Green. Come on."

"It's the birthplace of our freedom, for Christ's sake," Mundi said.

"Come on, don't give me a hard time. I hear that argument all day. Come on. Finish the coffee somewhere else or toss it in the trash. Come on, folks."

Smith said, "Show him your cookie cutter."

Mundi produced his badge and showed it to the officer. The officer started in on some small talk, and Smith and Mundi deadpanned him.

Smith drank coffee and went on. " . . .So finally the yuppies settle on my friend's aunt and bought a puppy from her. Then, a few months later, they call her back and say they want their money back because the dog had turned Godzilla on them. So she said fine, just bring the dog back to her and it can live on the farm. So the fuckin' yuppies said they couldn't because they'd put the puppy down."

"You gotta be shittin' me," Mundi said.

"Nope. And you know why they killed it?" Smith waited for Mundi to shake. "You know why? They said the dog was crazy because it jumped and barked a lot. It didn't know how to act proper around visitors."

"It was a fuckin' puppy. That's what puppies do. Particularly labs. They love to be comfortable. It's a known fact."

"You don't have to tell me. I fuckin' know. Just society in general. Those lazy bastards didn't have a clue how to raise a dog, so they kill it and then want their money back. Probably interfered with their schedules. They're worried about the dog's background and they're the ones screwed up, for Christ's sake," Smith said.

"It's true. I think it's the way people are raised today. I mean, look at that kid over there. Bellbottoms—tie-dye shirt. His parents are just reliving the 60's through him. Product of open campus. When we were kids we stole, smoked, swore, drank, and whatever else went with it, but I tell you something, we always said please and thank you," Mundi said.

"No kidding. All they do is spend time behind computers and then drink coffee on the sidewalk with their friends and complain about the burdens of life. I saw a kid the other day with pants so goddamn big, he had a skateboard in his pocket. I seriously don't know what's going to happen."

"I tell you, I give this country another twenty years," Mundi said. "Let's finish these coffees and talk to the arresting officer. What's the guy's name again?"

Smith drank the rest of her coffee and then lit a cigarette. "Jacobs," she said, "Susan Jacobs. Let's grab an early lunch. Place called Mario's down the center. Food's pretty good."

"Italian?" asked Mundi.

"Irish-German."

Had Mundi known that Smith was a dog lover, he might have taken care of those swollen glands earlier.

JOE GLEASON PICKED up the Red Line at Alewife Subway Station in North Cambridge and got off at Park Street, where he took the Green Line to Copley. Any doubts he had had about being a country lawyer in his hometown gave way as soon as he stepped on the train at Alewife like he was in a herd of cattle.

While he was on the subway, Joe saw an old man sitting across from him open a can of sardines, dump the contents onto a slice of bread, and make a sandwich. The old man ate the sandwich with his knees spread apart and let the olive oil dripping from the sandwich fall onto the subway car's floor. When he was done eating, he looked down at the floor and took notice of the mess he'd made. He addressed the situation by smearing the oil around with the soles of his boots before alighting at Central Square. Everyone had a face in mind, but no one said a word.

ON NEWBURY STREET in Boston, Gleason pulled a glass door open halfway when—from what seemed like nowhere—a huge hand finished the job for him. Gleason made a quick study of the man and saw that his lower lip was stitched and that he looked like he was still wearing his previous night's attire. The banged-up guy was pleasant, Joe thought.

"Go ahead," the Big Man said, sweeping an arm.

"Thanks," Joe said.

Joe stepped onto the quarry tile floor in the foyer and then the Big Man exited, heading down Newbury Street in the direction of the Boston Public Garden.

Gleason chose the stairs over the elevator and climbed up to the third floor of Cutter & Dudley. He expected to be greeted by some familiar faces. He had forgotten about attrition.

❖ ❖

NINETEEN

THE LAW OFFICES of Cutter & Dudley, LLP contained the proper Bostonian names, but most of the Brahmin stock had been thinned out a quarter of a century ago.

The firm was founded by two Harvard Law School graduates, Ernest Cutter and Ephraim Dudley, about two weeks after the death of Queen Victoria. About a year after the firm organized, Cutter died of influenza, and Dudley kept the firm going. There wasn't an employee at Cutter & Dudley who knew a thing about Cutter. In fact, the firm's archives don't even have a picture of him. During World War II, the firm went bankrupt and a couple of venture attorneys purchased the name of the firm to keep it a going concern.

Present day, Irish, Italians, Jews, Greeks, African Americans, and Hispanics run the firm, but with a fourth-generation Dudley still on the letterhead, the old money and people of design still feel safe there. Family secrets and all, old blood is good blood.

Lawrence Kennedy is the firm's street fighter. The higher reaches know nothing of him unless it's time to deal with the oddities associated with idle hands. The wills and trusts and bond floating side of the firm must also have its family secrets.

Gleason informed the woman at the desk who he was, and she rang Lawrence Kennedy's paralegal, who came out momentarily to collect Joe.

Kennedy didn't bother with formalities. "So you passed the bar and went out on your own," he said. "That takes some balls." Kennedy held his hand out and cupped it as if he was holding a set.

"I tell ya, Larry, I thought I had it all figured out. Good client base, some business skills, thought I knew the law—"

"And you read all the Mr. Tutt stories," Kennedy quipped.

"Read all the Tutt's and thought I had a grip on the human element, but there's always some new personality you fall for."

Kennedy got serious and put on his confiding look. "It doesn't end, Joe. Someone's always gonna come along and stick it to you. You get burned? You in trouble? Fall into a trap for the unwary?"

"I've got an ethical one for you. A moral question."

"Ouch," Kennedy said. "Moral victories don't get you a bowl game."

Kennedy's face was red, a healthy red, and his chin was one a king might envy.

"So, what's your ethical question, Joe? I'm sorry, moral question."

"Okay, a guy walks into my office with a collection case that's already marked up for bankruptcy, and I tell him that it's not worth it for me or him to chase."

"How much?"

"Three grand, but that's not my question. You see, shortly after this guy speaks to me, a contractor in Brighton gets knocked around and ends up dying."

"So you think once your client learned he had no practical legal remedy available to him, he took matters into his own hands? And you have a guilty conscience because you turned him off? And moreover, you think your advice led to the beating?"

"I'm wrestling with that, and also, what happens if I'm ever asked if I know anything about it?"

"Do you? For sure? You've surmised, Joe. Listen; think of ethics in a temporal sense. If a client has told you something in confidence that he has already done something illegal—then consider it privileged. If it's something he's going to do, or is in the process of doing, then it's likely it won't be a privileged communication. For example, if you get a client you know is a fugitive and he calls you up and starts to tell you where he is, stop him immediately."

"Why?"

"Because if you're asked by the authorities where your client is, you'd have to tell them since your client is a fugitive and in the process of committing a crime by being so. But keep in mind; you have no duty to volunteer. In your case, based on what you told me, your client has told you nothing about the alleged events. I don't see where you have a duty to report this. In fact, I think if you do, you've violated your client's privileged communication."

"Christ, I know all this and yet I can't figure out why it bothers me so much. When I was in law school, I thought I could separate the law and my own personal beliefs, but I can't."

"You'll kill yourself if you don't, Joe; your family, too. There are certain horrors you're going to be privy to in this business: some to ignore, some to defend, maybe some to judge. You'll become like a fuckin' priest. You'll see just how screwed up and sick people can be. You'll start to see shit you just can't make up: Mothers sleeping with sons. Screwing dead animals. The world is a house of horrors. Just a giant fiddle fuck fest."

"Yeah. So much for being a country lawyer."

A pause.

Kennedy said, "This guy a friend of yours?"

"Yeah. A guy I sanded floors with during law school."

"I heard you're still knocking down floors. O'Kane Hardwood Floors. That the company?"

"Yeah. I'll work with them once in a while," Gleason said. "Need some physical work. One form of work nurtures the other, I keep telling myself."

"That's good, just to get you out of the office now and then. Listen; don't be like me, getting stuck in the big firm route. You did the smart thing going on your own, trust me. I'm sixty-eight, Joe, and I'm finding more and more that I have to stand up in court to many of the people who used to work for me. Little by little, you'll not only build the client base, but you'll build the wheels you need to handle their problems. I told you before, if you get any cases you need help on, you can come in here and work them up with me as co-counsel. If you need money, Joe—"

"Listen, I get by okay. I always find a way to make a few bucks and stay current with the bills."

"I'd take you back in a minute, Joe. If you want to do a year or two here, you could, but I just don't want you to get sucked in. Think about it. It would get you a base outside your circle. Working for friends and family is tough sledding."

Gleason balanced that last utterance of Kennedy's with the thought of daily public transportation, and the

123

man with the sardine sandwich came to mind. Something about Kennedy's proposition didn't pass the smell test.

"Sure," Gleason said, "I'll think about it."

"Let me get a couple of your cards."

From his inside coat pocket, Gleason removed a black leather wallet that Maria had given him after graduating from law school, and handed Kennedy a few cards.

"Nice wallet," Kennedy said.

Gleason slid it back into his inside breast pocket and patted the wallet. "Yeah, but I guess it's what's inside that counts."

Kennedy saw Gleason to the outside, and on the way back to his office, his paralegal handed him a pink slip with a telephone number on it. Kennedy recognized the number, but didn't do anything with it right away.

IN HIS OFFICE Lawrence Kennedy leaned back in his leather chair and looked at his grandfather's Bachelor of Laws diploma from Suffolk Law School.

His grandfather, Stephen A. Kennedy, was first-generation Irish and one of four high school students to be accepted at the Cambridge Latin School (the nursery of Harvard men) for a special program that gave him an opportunity to attend high school there as long as he completed the program in four years instead of the mandatory five. Despite losing fifty percent of his hearing to scarlet fever as a boy, Kennedy's grandfather was the only one of the four given the challenge who met it successfully.

At the graduation ceremony, no mention was made of his feat as the only person ever to complete the five-year program in four years (this at an age of seventeen). No mention at all! After all, he was from Irish stock.

124

After high school graduation in 1906, he took the Harvard entrance exams and was accepted. His future was mapped out for him until a week before freshman year, when his father succumbed to the injuries he had sustained some four decades earlier in the Civil War. Stephen's opportunity to attend Harvard vanished with his father's death. Years later Stephen discovered that scholarships had been available to him, something his instructors in high school had neglected to tell him.

He went on, however, to become paymaster for United Rexall. Sometime in August 1914, Stephen was walking around Roxbury during his lunch break when he saw an old house with a sign hanging in the window that read: "Archer's Evening Law School." Taking interest in the notice, he entered the house and spoke with Dean Archer, who informed Stephen that the school couldn't confer a degree, but if it was enrichment he was after, he had come to the right place.

Stephen enrolled, and by 1918 the school had moved to Mount Vernon Street, changed its name to Suffolk Law School, and was, by that time, able to confer Bachelor of Laws degrees to its graduates. It was the same year he graduated.

Kennedy recalled that all his grandfather ever really wanted was to make a better life for his children. He looked around his law office and thought of the powerful cronies he had, saw how much he had and how much he could do without even leaving his law office. Sometimes all he had to do was walk down the corridor of a courthouse, but he was still an outsider in his firm. For some reason he wasn't from the right cut. Had his grandfather made it to Harvard, things might have been different but not necessarily better. Things might have been tougher in his grandfather's day, but they were much simpler too.

In addition to graduating law school in 1918, Kennedy's grandfather lost a set of twins to the influenza epidemic that same year.

Generations removed from the pains associated with a simpler life, the grass is always greener.

TWENTY

LAWRENCE KENNEDY PICKED up the receiver to his phone and dialed the number his paralegal had given him. He knew it wasn't good news.

"Senator Custance's office," a pleasant voice answered.

"Attorney Lawrence Kennedy returning the Senator's call," Kennedy said.

"Just a moment, I'll see if he's in."

The Senator's voice came over the line. "Counselor, how are things?"

"Just fine, Dick. I'm sorry about Elizabeth. I've been meaning to get out to your place."

"Thank God for work. It's what keeps me going. Listen, I'm calling about your new client."

"Okay?" Kennedy knew the Senator meant the Big Man and that it was time to start speaking in general terms.

"I'm upset about what happened to him, and I just hope he has the best defense available."

"You know he has that, Senator."

"Good, because I think someone with a substance problem shouldn't have to face prosecution. He or she should receive treatment, not punishment."

"I see, Senator, but you know I can never make any guarantees."

"Make me one in this case, will you? As a favor to a long-time supporter? Did I hear something about you putting in for a judgeship? I think the corner office could use a little prodding."

The offer of a judgeship was worth a guarantee.

"You know I like to guarantee my work, Senator. My best to the governor."

Custance had enough political juice on the Hill so that he wasn't someone you let down, particularly if you planned to remain at Cutter & Dudley or if you ever expected to be a judge. With a million-and-a-half dollar home in Weston, a thirty-five-year-old wife—his third—and two kids with the Harvard B School laid out as goals, Kennedy's monthly expenses required his bi-monthly nut from the firm.

"As always, Senator, your passion for assisting the unfortunate is something Cutter & Dudley looks forward to advancing."

"Thanks, Lawrence. This is something the less fortunate won't forget." The Senator disconnected the line.

Kennedy looked back up at his grandfather's diploma and thought about what Joe Gleason had told him about the McDermott attack in Brighton. He could use it to leverage the Middlesex DA. Swap a murder for an OUI.

He walked out of his office and said to his paralegal, "See if a prosecutor named Jan Storrow is still up at Concord District Court. If not, get me her office."

❖

"JAN STORROW," THE voice said. It was Nose Job.

"Jan, Lawrence Kennedy. I spoke to you this morning in connection with the Big Man."

"Of course. What can I do for you? I told you I have my marching orders."

"I know you do. I'm calling on another matter. There was a fellow beaten to death in Brighton. I think a few weeks back. I think if someone from Suffolk County gets in touch with O'Kane Hardwood Floors, they may be able to turn something up."

"And what do you want in return—a CWOF for the Big Man?"

"I don't want a thing. I'll leave it to your sense of fair play and substantial justice. I'm just being a helpful citizen. My civic duty. Of course, if you think a CWOF is what the Commonwealth wants, I'm sure we can sew things up at pretrial."

"Let me make some calls to Suffolk. Lexington will hate to lose this one. Best copy they've had since the Revolution. And, like I said, I've got my marching orders," Storrow said.

"Right," Kennedy said, "We all get them once in a while, Counselor."

Kennedy looked up at his grandfather's diploma. He felt a painful tug in his groin. He didn't trust Storrow and had a feeling that once she looked into his background, she'd be tempted to stay in and not offer much up. He rang his legal assistant and ordered a little insurance.

"Terry, get on the horn to Concord District and tell them we'll need a Portuguese interpreter on the Big Man file, okay?"

"Okay," She hung up and sighed.

SNAFU: Situation Normal, All Fucked Up. Once again, no lunch today for dutiful, yet hungry Terry.

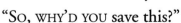

"So, WHY'D YOU save this?"

"Evidence."

"Evidence?"

129

"Evidence."

"Okay, evidence," Mundi said. "Why did you save this important piece of evidence, Sergeant?"

"Because it's evidence," Sergeant Jacobs of the Lexington Police Department said, referring to the lottery scratch ticket that the Big Man had purchased at Benson's Diner in Wayland. It was sealed in a small plastic bag and labeled Exhibit D. There was moisture build-up against the inside wall of the bag.

"Why is it evidence?" Mundi asked.

"Because it's soaked in booze. Booze he purchased in Concord by the wheelbarrow full with a stack of new twenties. The Big Man busted a bottle of Johnnie Walker Red during his joy ride, and it splashed all over the ticket. I want to put open booze at the scene. You see evidence can disappear over time. It's oftentimes evanescent. You have to capture it—keep it fresh—keep it alive. Get hold of it and preserve it before it's gone. You see what I'm saying, folks?"

Mundi nodded several times and then handed the evidence bag to Smith.

"This is a thousand dollar winner," Smith said.

"His lucky day," Jacobs returned. "He bought it at a place called Benson's in Wayland."

"How d'ya know?" Smith asked.

"Track number on the ticket. I placed a telephone call to the Massachusetts State Lottery. They keep track of where every ticket is sold."

"I know—but why did you find that out?" Smith asked.

"Wanted to know where he was. To see if he was at a place he could get loaded. Why are you guys into this?"

Jacobs asked.

"Because," Mundi said while pointing his index finger at the sergeant, "justice demands it. When I stood on the Battle Green not more than sixty minutes ago, I recalled the message our forebears fought and died for over two centuries ago. They spilled blood on that Green so that future generations could live in peace and express their views without the fear of reprisal from a bastard king. I'm doing this for all the folks who believe in advancing the cause of justice, brotherhood, sisterhood, love, good-will toward all, and maybe just a good old-fashioned pat on the back when a friend is feeling a bit down. I love this country. I've sworn before God to uphold not only the Constitution of the United States of America, but also the Massachusetts Declaration of Rights, which, by the way, is the oldest constitution in the world, and anyone who attempts to run roughshod over these instruments, which so many have died for, is going to have to get through me first, damn it."

"Yeah," Smith said, "yeah."

Smith and Mundi marched out of the Lexington Police Station in unison as if they were Sean Connery and Michael Caine in "The Man Who Would Be King."

A Sean Connery fan, too. Mundi would have taken care of those swollen glands, had he known.

TWENTY-ONE

MUNDI AND SMITH walked into Benson's Diner in Wayland. Mundi took it.

"Jack Mundi, Special Omnibus Detective, Boston," Mundi said to the cook who had served the Big Man. "This is Reva Smith, also Special Omnibus." He held up a picture of the Big Man and showed it to the cook. "Have you seen this man?"

The cook wiped his hands on his apron and then decided against holding the picture. He just bent his thin frame over the counter and into the picture with a clever tilt to his head. His English suddenly got good. "Yes. I have seen that man before. We often make fun of him."

"What d'ya mean 'we'? You're the only one here. What are you saying? I don't see anyone else. Come clean, boyo. Who's the 'we'? Are you hiding something? Who's the 'we'? Who is it? Because you're working here alone, from what I see. Smith, is he alone?"

"Alone, Detective," Smith answered, standing akimbo and chewing gum as fast as she could.

"Listen," the cook said, "my sister—"

"Your sister!" Mundi yelled. "Is she sleeping with this crap? Enough of your choplogic. Are you insane, letting her even come near this bastard? This man is sick in the fucking head! He's the Devil's asshole. I'll slap a writ of death knell on this place so goddamn fast no one will ever get through that door again, pal. Now, what's going on here?"

"We—" the cook began, "I mean, my sister works here with me sometimes. The guy was funny, that's all.

He made a big thing about potato chips, so I remembered him. Another guy came in and sat down with him. A funny little guy."

"What did the little funny guy look like?" Mundi said.

"Funny *little* guy. Not little funny guy," Smith corrected, leading with her jaw.

"He was old. I'd say in his sixties, gray hair, and clothes too big. Kinda messy looking guy with big black glasses; a creepy smile. Looked like one of those guys who worked in the house and never got out or something. All matted down kinda."

"Yeah, you got a good eye for detail, boyo. Did you pull a tail job on them after their meeting?"

The kid showed the palms of his hands. "You mean did I follow them? No."

"I'm going to report that, and I'm also going to get to the bottom of the missing quart of strawberries . . .I know a duplicate key existed," Mundi said, and then turned to Smith with one eye still on the cook. His lips were tight. "You got any questions, Ninety-Nine?"

"Yeah, Thirteen," Smith said. "Cheeseburgers come with fries or chips?"

RETURNING TO BOSTON, Smith asked Mundi, "Are you still pissed at me, Jack?"

Mundi's arms were folded, and he just looked out the passenger's window without responding.

"You know, Jack," Smith said, "silence is a form of abuse."

"Well, you shouldn't have done it then. That was abuse too, and any judge would agree with me."

"Look, I'm sorry."

Mundi lifted a hand. "Forget it. It's all right."

"That's not good enough. You don't sound sincere. I want this issue to pass without affecting our relationship. I've learned a lot about myself today"

"You know something? Women should run the fuckin' world. Because we'd never have a war again. We'd only have 'issues.' Well, the issue is this . . .if I call you Ninety-Nine, then I'm Eighty-Six and not Thirteen. That was a cheap shot."

"That was a cheap shot, and I apologize."

"Okay. Apology accepted. Now, let's get back. The Chief wants to see us back at Control."

THE CHIEF MOVED from side to side in his vinyl swivel and was nipping at a red delicious apple with his incisors. He thought he'd selected a good one, but it turned out to be mealy. A chunk fell off the apple and rolled over a few tie moguls. He made a face.

"I thought you were dead or something like that?" the Chief said to Mundi.

"Not yet, sir. Those reports were greatly exaggerated, if I can steal one from Twain. Anyway, there's been a hold-up. Something to do with the Consolidated Omnibus Budget Reconciliation Act."

"What?"

"COBRA benefits, sir."

"Oh." He turned to Smith and asked, "And what's your story?"

Smith shook her head. She had a headache. She had drunk a six-pack of a dark micro brew the night before, and the chicken with parm she'd had for lunch was

134

conspiring. That was it . . . . The last time . . . . Never again
. . . . No more micro brew.

The Chief attacked his apple and played with his
palate for a few moments with his tongue. The moment
Smith heard that spanking sound, she knew she was married to it for the rest of the day.

"I like to eat my apples around in a circle," the
Chief then said, "and see how thin I can make the bridge.
See what I mean?"

The Chief held the apple in front of Smith and
Mundi. There was a thin red sliver that separated the bite
marks. One small nip and there would be a free flow of
bites around the apple.

"I do," Mundi nodded. "I do. I see what you
mean. You've made that path of skin very thin indeed.
You really have."

"You have," Smith said. She gave a conferring nod
to Mundi too. "I couldn't do that. My teeth are too
thick."

"I eat right and I'm still fat," the Chief said. He
let out air. "Anyway, you two have been kind of scarce,
haven't you?"

"What do you mean?" Mundi said.

"Usually you're fucking off, only you do it around
here where I can keep an eye on you. Where you been all
day?"

Smith shrugged.

Mundi shrugged.

"So, neither one of you knows where you've
been?"

Mundi's head dropped. Smith just looked at a
mug full of pencils on the Chief's desk. It was a frog mug.

The Chief collected froggy things, and they were all over the office. The chief ran his tongue over his teeth.

"Mundi, where you been?" he asked.

"I don't know. Just been doing things. You know."

"Smith?"

Smith moved her head back and forth.

"I don't know," she said. "It's like he said. We didn't do nothing. We were just out, that's all."

The Chief looked at his apple. It was starting to turn brown.

"I don't buy one word of it. From either one of you. Neither of you would say shit if you had it in your mouth, anyway. Now, you two guys get the hell out of here."

They got up to leave, and as they were exiting the office, the Chief said to Mundi, "Mundi, take care of that cobra snake thing and get back to me by the end of next week if you're still alive."

"Right, Chief."

Outside the office Smith asked, "What's less apt to cause a headache, draft beer or bottled?"

"Bottled. Both are tough on the kidneys. And stay away from aged cheese. The tyramine in it can cause headaches, according to Doctor Seymour Diamond."

"Right," Smith said, and then walked away taking some, but not all, of her scent with her.

TWENTY-TWO

TRIAL COURT OF THE COMMONWEALTH
DISTRICT COURT DEPARTMENT, WALTHAM
DIVISION
WALTHAM, MASSACHUSETTS

"You know anything about hanging curtains?"
Gleason asked the prosecutor.

"Not really. Why?"

"I gotta get a curtain up on my office door. People
can look in the window when I have a client."

"The first thing you have to do is measure the
window."

"I did that. I went all the way to the goddamn
hardware store and that's the first thing the lady asks me,
so I had to go back and do it. The problem now is that
the door is one of those new metal insulated things and I
don't want to bang nails into it. I don't know how to get
the curtain rod fastened to it without putting holes into
the door."

"Yeah, that is a tough one. I don't know what to
say. Are there any suction cup things you can use?"

"There must be something. I've been meaning to
take care of it for a year and just never got around to it.
Oh well."

"Hey, I've been meaning to ask you, Joe, why do
you have a Canadian flag license plate?"

"Bobby Orr's from Canada."

The prosecutor accepted the answer.

Gleason paused. "So what can we do?"

"I haven't even read the file. Can I give you any leeway here?"

"I brought him in on a surrender," Gleason said. "He was pulled over for failure to keep right some time last July and it turns out his vehicle was unregistered. On arraignment he was let go on his own recognizance and told to appear, but he ends up defaulting. Just a kid and thought it would fall through the cracks, ya know? Now he wants to make sure his ass isn't hanging out, so I brought him in."

"Get the default lifted?" the prosecuting officer asked.

"Yeah."

"Probation recall the warrant?"

"Yeah. I'd like to button this up first call. It's a first offense."

The prosecuting officer scribbled down what his recommendation would be to the judge, and handed it to Joe. He said, "We'll just fine him and not enter a guilty plea. Filing fee of a hundred and fifty bucks."

"You guys should just set up a cash register here."

The officer smiled and said, "Can he pay it today?"

"His mother's here."

"That a 'yes.'"

"yep."

❖

MARIA GLEASON WAS inspecting the pillow that Tony Vaccaro's grandmother had made at Joe Gleason's request. The Wallflowers' "Sixth Avenue Heartache" was coming through on a clock radio.

"Where'd you get this?" Maria asked. "This is

138

really nice. I love the colors."

"I got it from a nun."

"A nun?"

"Yeah. I bought it from a nun. You know, the nuns who make pillows up at the Gray Nuns."

"Nuns who make pillows?"

"Yeah. I mean, they make other things like mittens, and First Communion bibs, but primarily pillows for people who don't have any."

"I see," Maria said. "First Communion bibs? Baptismal bibs, maybe?"

"Those too," Joe said.

She went over to the chair he was sitting in and hit him on the crown of his head with the pillow.

"You're up to something," she said.

"I'm just trying to save America," Joe said.

Another hit on the crown.

INDIAN SUMMER MELTED the snow that had fallen just a few days earlier. The window box displaying variegated euonymus across from 22B West Cedar Street on Beacon Hill still thrived, and so did the hearty white mums in the peat pot by Tick Dillon's feet. It was a 2.4 million dollar address—not home—and it wasn't Yankee money, it was yuppie credit.

Jim O'Kane said he was running down some estimates and left Tick on the job. Tick knew O'Kane was out playing a round of golf and that it was the sweat of Tick's brow that put him there. Tick was starting to get the joke.

Tick dropped his cigarette on the brick sidewalk consisting of Boston City Pavers and extinguished it with his Die Hards. The soles of his boots wore fine, but the toes were worn through from rubbing against the hardwood while he scraped down the corners and thresholds on his hands and knees. Boots—another hundred bucks.

He went into 22B and started wrapping up the cord to the edger. His Nextel beeped, and he responded to his boss, Jim O'Kane.

"Hello, Jim."

"Tick, how far are you?"

"Ready to buff it out."

"What do you think?" O'Kane asked.

"Go with a hundred grit."

"New or used?"

"New."

"Go with a used eighty then. There's a whole stack in the van."

"Right."

"You going to get a coat on that today?"

"Emm—getting late. I gotta meet Mary. She's been on my case, said she's got to have a talk with me."

"Okay, listen. Just get me set up for coating then. I might swing in there tonight. You can drop the van back at my place."

"Listen, Jim, what should I do with the bags of dust? I can't just leave 'em here."

"Toss 'em in the back of the van. I want those floors looking like furniture, Tick."

There was a full-length mirror in the basement covering a good portion of a brick wall, and Tick looked at himself as he buffed a small section of maple floor next to a bar. The rubber straps from the dust masks he'd been wearing on the job for five years were starting to make permanent impressions in his face. The fine sawdust sucked all the moisture out of his hands, and during the winter months the joints of his fingers and thumbs split and cracked. They were starting to look like his father's hands. Mostly, he watched his eyes and just wondered who he was. He was alone too much.

Before vacuuming the dust raised from screening the floors, Tick had a cigarette out front. He smoked it halfway and dropped it on the front landing. He stepped on it but didn't knock out the whole head.

He strapped the vacuum to his back and began vacuuming the floors. On his way out, he vacuumed the cigarette butts he had left in front of 22B, including the one that still smoldered.

He pulled the used bag out of the vacuum, tossed it into a bag of sawdust, tied the top of the bag together, and then threw it into the back of the van with several other trash bags.

JOE GLEASON MET Tony Vaccaro at a job site in Wakefield.

"What's up?" Vaccaro asked.

"Not much. How's your grandmother doing?"

"Not bad."

"Okay, listen, get her some more yarn for me, okay? Get it up there today and tell her I'm still doing some research."

"Who's the pillow for this time?"

"It's a surprise, Brudda," Gleason said.

A 1987 ONE ton Ford dump truck pulled up to the site and the high school drop out working for Vaccaro stepped out of the truck with a plastic bottle of Coke and a paper bag containing a meatball sub.

Vaccaro reached for his belt, pressed a button and noted the time from his pager.

"You know," Vaccaro said to the high school drop out, "you only got three minutes to eat that sub."

The helper's mouth was open with thought. "I thought I get a half hour for lunch?"

"And it took you twenty-seven minutes to pick it up. That's part of your lunch. I'm not paying you to run out to lunch and then come back and eat it."

The helper let his shoulders drop and he let out a long sigh. He was in for a long life.

MARY BOYLE WAS waiting for Tick to stop bouncing a tennis ball off the floor into his hand. He was smoking a cigarette and the smoke was getting into his eyes, but he refused to remove it from his mouth. She grew tired of waiting and tried to get in what she had to announce in between bounces.

"We need to talk," she said.

"We do?"

"Yes, we do. Stop bouncing the ball, Tick."

He began bouncing it faster and faster. When he lost control of it, he got up and began kicking it around the kitchen. When he finally had control of it in his hand, he wound up and threw it into a stack of dishes in the sink.

Mary's left hand made an awning over her eyes.

After a few rapid hauls off his cigarette, Tick sat down and said, "So, what do you need to discuss that's so important I needed to miss work this evening? I need every hour I can get!"

"You mean like the hours you spend down the pub and the hours you spend sleeping it off. You must know I'm pregnant."

"I wouldn't know that. How the fuck would I know that? I'm asking you, Mary, how in Christ's name would I know that?"

Mary's face was red. She wiped away her tears. "I don't believe you. I don't even know why I bother or even have you around."

"Now don't start. If a man doesn't work hard, he's a bum, and if he does, he's never around. We can't win. There's no pleasing you people."

"Don't turn this into something it isn't," Mary said. "I'm telling you I'm pregnant and that you're responsible."

Tick mashed out his cigarette into a saucer with some egg white in it, and got out of his chair to walk around the kitchen. From the refrigerator he pulled out a Budweiser and twisted the cap.

"I never said I wasn't responsible, Mary. I just can't get married. I can't be like Joe Gleason. He got married and it turned out the thing died anyway. Now he's stuck."

"What do you mean stuck?"

"Well, he can't get divorced, can he?"

"Maybe he doesn't want to," Mary said.

"Don't drag me into this. You don't know what Joe wants, Mary."

"Neither do you. You're the one who brought him up."

"The point I'm trying to make is," Tick said, "I'll

stand by you, but I'm not getting married until I'm ready. It's the best for everybody. The baby and everybody, and that's the end of the conversation. Now have you been to see a doctor?"

He was reaching for a cigarette when Mary got up and started to leave.

Tick raised his voice. "I say are you getting proper nourishment? Have you been to see a doctor?"

Mary turned around. "I can handle this alone, Tick. I just thought you might like to know that you're responsible."

He finished lighting his menthol and said, "Well, fine, I know now. And I know my responsibilities."

Mary donned her coat and then left. Tick revisited the refrigerator and when that was done, it was the pub.

TWENTY-THREE

WHILE PARKED OUTSIDE the Big Man's apartment on Commonwealth Avenue, in Boston's Back Bay, detective Smith was working on getting her head into a comfortable position when Mundi said, "She didn't throw it back, she threw it into her carriage."

"You sure? I always thought she threw it back onto the meat rack."

"No. I used to think that too, but she threw it into her shopping carriage."

"I wish I could ride a horse," Smith said. "They say a horse can always tell if you rode."

"Really?"

"Yeah. It's a known fact."

"What's your favorite western?" Mundi asked.

"Not even a contest. 'Shane.' Good book too. Read it in seventh grade."

"That was a book, too?"

"Great book. Little guy against the big guy. You gotta love it when the little guy wins. What's your favorite?"

"'True Grit,'" Mundi said.

"That was okay. I'm glad the Duke got the Oscar for that, but it wasn't his best."

"How many times did you see it?"

"Just once," Smith said.

"I felt the same way when I saw it the first time, but it's one of those movies you gotta see a few times to appreciate."

"Maybe I'll rent that this weekend. I could go for

a good Duke movie," Smith said.

"You know Dennis Hopper was in it?"

"Really?"

"Yep. He had a ponytail," Mundi said.

"Glenn Campbell was in it, wasn't he?"

"Right. And Jimmy Stewart and Ron Howard—No. Wait a minute," Mundi said correcting himself, "that was 'The Shootist.' The Duke's last movie. You like country?"

"Not really. Couldn't live on it."

"It's all right."

"Smells like sour milk around here," Smith said.

"Yeah, it does. But at least it's better than when that farm turned over their compost pile in Lexington."

"Was that the smell?"

"Think so."

"I'd take car exhaust over that crap," Smith said. She wiped away breath off the driver's window. She watched as a woman wearing only a black bra for a top flagged down a taxi. "I could have sworn Mary Tyler Moore threw the steak back on the meat rack."

"I'm telling you, she threw it in her carriage," Mundi said. "Swear to God . . .I'm pretty sure, anyway."

❖

THAT EVENING JIM O'Kane went to 22B West Cedar Street to put on the first coat of polyurethane. What O'Kane called a sealer coat, which consisted of seventy percent oil-based polyurethane and thirty percent thinner. An explosive concoction, but it cut costs.

He had waited for traffic to die down and headed in around seven-thirty under a harvest moon. What Native Americans used to call a Beaver Moon. By nine-

146

thirty he had the floors coated and the van packed and ready to leave West Cedar. The Kinvara Pub in Brighton was his next destination.

Near Fenway Park, he started to smell smoke coming from the back of the van. "Fall on Me" by R.E.M. was playing on the radio. He pulled into a taxi stand by O'Keefe's Funeral Home and, after putting the van into park, slid open a door in between the two front seats that led from the cabin of the van to the back. In the back of the van he felt around for a flashlight, and when he located one, flashed it on the bags Dillon had left in the back. He opened a few and shook them a bit to see if he could locate where the smoke was coming from.

The sawdust from floor sanding is like powder. Like the coal dust from a mine, it becomes airborne when disturbed, and in the right conditions it can combust. The dust was starting to fill the back of the van. Finally, O'Kane opened a bag and shook it. That fed a small stash of cinders the oxygen it needed to ignite.

"Ahh, Tick, you fuck," he said to himself, "you vacuumed up a cigarette."

While he was looking for something to douse the ashes with, a cloud of dust combusted in the bag and then ignited the airborne dust. As if it was shot out of the barrel of a cannon, a flame front launched O'Kane into the back of the van door, which was locked on the outside. A red metal box, containing brushes soaking in thinner, tipped over and rolled toward O'Kane. A blue and red flame swallowed it whole.

Instinctively he burrowed into a corner and tried to kick away the flames, only fanning their anger. Fire engulfed his escape hatch back into the cabin. His eyebrows and the hair on his arms were already singed off completely. Seeing his predicament, he started kicking the flames again. The combustion had eaten most of the oxygen in the van, and he was finding it difficult to breathe. The heat burned his lungs the way deep breathes in a sauna do. The fire quickly lapped up any oxygen that did come in through the seams of the van.

Like a turned-over crab, he desperately tried to swat the fire away with his hands and legs, but the back of the van was in full conflagration.

At first it was his screams of horror that drew a small sidewalk crowd, but when fire could be seen from the outside, the crowd multiplied. A sealed bucket containing polyurethane and thinner exploded. Someone eventually called 911, while the van's radio still played.

Not long after Jim O'Kane's body let out its final hisses in the envelope of fire, the book of matches in his left breast pocket ignited into quick, distinct illumination, and that was the end of Jim O'Kane.

TWENTY-FOUR

"WHAT TIME IS it? This clock right?" Smith asked.

She and Mundi were still on obo in front of the Big Man's brownstone on Commonwealth Avenue.

"Minute ahead of my watch. Nine forty's about right. I meant to ask you—why don't you carry a watch?"

"Just don't like them. You know. The metal bands pull your hair out and the leather straps get all sweaty and smelly. I wish it was like the old days—I'd carry a pocket watch," Smith said.

"Women didn't have pocket watches," Mundi said.

"Bullshit. Sharon Stone did in 'The Quick and the Dead.'"

"Did she? That would be great. I think if I could live anytime, it would be the 1890's."

"No way," Smith said. "I think probably like the early 1800s and go on a whaling ship."

"Well, that's what's good about the 1890s. You could still go whaling and at the same time medicine was better. So if you had to get a tooth out or an appendix, they'd probably have a painkiller. I think they had aspirin in the 1890s."

"Well, you could just drink rum or something to kill the pain."

"Yeah, but with all that alcohol, you might bleed too much," Mundi said.

"I read somewhere that someday people won't have wisdom teeth. I wasn't born with any."

149

"I was. Actually, I was born with only three. I had those taken out. Wasn't too bad, but I wouldn't want to go through that again."

"My theory is that, if you're born without wisdom teeth, then you're genetically superior."

"Okay. Why's that, Nietzsche?" Mundi said.

"Well," thus spoke Smith, "it just makes sense. You see, the reason we had wisdom teeth is that, in the olden days, people would lose their teeth, more often than not leaving gaps. The wisdom teeth come in early adulthood to replace the ones lost. But now we take better care of our teeth and we don't lose them as much. The reason wisdom teeth need to be taken out is because there's no room for them. So over time our bodies are rewriting our DNA saying, 'Hey we don't need that wisdom teeth gene anymore. Get rid of it.' The bodies that have advanced have already done that. Like mine."

"So you're saying I'm more of a caveman than you?"

"I guess so. And that's why I could go whaling in the early 1800s and not have to worry about getting my wisdom teeth yanked."

"Yeah, but that doesn't make sense."

"In what way?"

"Well, you presume you're genetically superior because you were born without wisdom teeth. Maybe it was a defect and not an advancement in genes. Just like some people are born without arms or legs," Mundi said.

"Hey, listen, you were born with only three wisdom teeth, so you're not doing too bad. That's better than most."

"I wonder if Sharon Stone was born with wisdom

teeth."

"Who cares? She carried a pocket watch. What time is it?" Smith asked.

Mundi and Smith heard O'Kane's fire come in from dispatch and responded after noting the time via Mundi's watch.

WHAT REMAINED OF Jim O'Kane was flown back to Shannon, Ireland, and then carted up to Omagh, where a father who hadn't seen or heard from his son in over a decade buried him.

There was no fiddle or tunes at Jim O'Kane's wake. His father didn't drink. He just found comfort in work and in trade, and in methods that gave him character to those passing through.

At Saint Columkille's on Market Street in Brighton, Tick arranged with the pastor to hold a service on behalf of Jim O'Kane, and afterward, everyone met up at The Village.

"Poor Tick," County Tyrone said.

"What's up?" City of Dublin asked.

"Maria's preggers."

"Shite," Dublin said. "Poor bastard; first O'Kane and now that cross to bear. Jesus, Mary, and Joseph."

Tyrone agreed. "Aye, surely. Awful thing, really."

"HEY," SMITH SAID.

"Hey," Mundi returned.

"That guy who got cooked the other night in the van turned out to be a suspect in the McDermott. The Suffolk DA got a tip."

"Really?"

"Really. Are we looking into it?"

"Sure. You're dying remember? We can do whatever we want."

"Me, not you."

"Bullshit. Once you die, I'll just blame everything on you."

Mundi thought for a moment. "There's a punch line there somewhere, I just can't think of one."

Smith started to leave. She turned around.

"Oh, by the way. I almost forgot," She said. "Guess who they got the tip from?"

"Charles Nelson Reilly?"

"Nope. Your buddy, Lawrence Kennedy."

MARY BOYLE WOULD co-operate with the authorities. She knew the consequences of not doing so. She had grown up in Belfast, Ireland, and when she was twelve, she saw her older brother, Paddy, get stopped for a routine shakedown by a British soldier. The soldier was eighteen and spread Paddy against an abandoned Toyota. Paddy made some wise remarks, and when the soldier backed up a bit, Paddy reached into his front pants pocket for a box of cigarettes. That was the last conscious move he ever made. The soldier buried three rounds into his back. He wasn't wearing any shirt. His blood percolated for a moment, and the battle was all over for him. The soldier did one year and then it was over for him. At the age of twelve, Mary Boyle was left to figure things out, told to forget about it, put it behind her.

To most of those who knew her, Mary Boyle seemed congenial to the point of being simple, with nothing underneath and with nothing along the way to put behind her.

❖

THE FLAGSTONE PATH led to a set of wooden steps on Bennett Street in Brighton. Mundi and Smith followed it, and when they reached the hunter green door, they knocked and announced. Mary Boyle answered.

"I'm Detective Jack Mundi and this is Detective Reva Smith. We'd like to speak with Mr. Patrick Dillon."

Mary presumed it was passport-related. Her eyes glazed over them with noticeable fear.

"He's away," Mary said.

"Where can we find him?" Smith asked.

"His friend died. He's away," Mary said after some thought.

"Is Jim O'Kane the friend who died?" Smith asked.

"Yes, but it was an accident. Tick didn't mean to start the fire. It can happen," she said. "I thought this was about his passport."

Smith looked confused, and Mundi caught it in time to take over.

"We figured that was all it was. We just wanted a routine statement, is all. Unless it was natural causes, we have to follow everything up. Can I get your name?"

"Mary Boyle."

"Thank you, Mary. Does Patrick live here?"

"He does."

"And he worked for Jim O'Kane . . .Is that how they knew each other?"

Mary rubbed her eyes. Her stomach turned.

"I don't know how they met. We all seem to fall together over here. Someone knows someone. You know

153

how it is."

"Now—just so I can get this down—Patrick told you this was an accident?"

"Yes. Tick's not even sure it was him. But he thinks it may have been one of his cigarette butts."

"Who's Tick?"

"Patrick. It's his nickname."

Smith wrote it down on a small notebook pad.

"Mind if we take a quick look around?"

"Emm, I don't."

Mary Boyle held her stomach. She was only three months pregnant, but she felt a painful stir. At this point she knew that she had said too much, yet she was afraid to turn back. Besides, she figured there was nothing to hide.

Smith and Mundi entered. The dwelling was dark and smelled like fried fish and stale tobacco. To their right was a living room, which a cursory inspection revealed to be unremarkable. Down the hall, the kitchen proved equally unremarkable.

"Can we just look at his room?" asked Smith.

Mary Boyle led them to her and Tick's room.

They looked around with no real objective in mind. Smith walked over to the nightstand and read the business card next to the telephone. "THE LAW OFFICE OF JOSEPH C. GLEASON."

"Well," Smith said to Mundi, "it looks like our little Irish lamb has got himself a lawyer."

Mundi took the card and read it. "He's a notary public too."

"Is this enough to go in with?"

"It looks that way, Detective. Let's pay a visit to

154

a neutral and detached magistrate and get ourselves an arrest warrant based on objective facts."

"Right," Smith said. "Objective facts . . .A neutral and detached magistrate. Better make it one we know."

"Right. We'd better."

TWENTY-FIVE

MARK TWAIN CONTENDED that naked people have little or no influence on society.

"That was a nice pillow you gave to your mother," Maria Gleason said as she walked into the bedroom from the shower. She had one towel twisted around her head and another around her trunk. "Crush" by the Dave Matthew's band was playing.

"Thanks," Joe said. He was lying in bed with an old pair of A-Team boxer shorts on.

"Get it from the same nun?"

"Yep."

"You're not going to tell me where you're getting these pillows, are you?"

"Nope."

"Why?"

"Confidential. Attorney-client privilege."

"You told me about Tick."

"That's because you worked down the office once in a while and were in my employ."

"I'm not in your employ anymore?"

"No, you're fired."

"What do I have to do to get my job back?"

"Return my towel."

Maria took the towel off her head, balled it up, and threw it at him.

Gleason inspected it.

"This is your towel."

She threw the second towel at him and, while naked, was taken back at Joe's firm.

156

❖

IT WAS SATURDAY, December 8, and Joe Gleason decided he'd address another envelope before taking his afternoon walk. He slid the envelope into his old IBM electric and spun it through. He had a computer that could address envelopes, but he could never seem to align the envelope so that the address printed straight.

He finished and pushed the piece aside so that he could inspect it with a clear head after his walk.

Cold air rushed through Jackson's Meadow and shot down the railroad tracks. Joe's mind weighed heavily with thought after thought. Just as he finished thinking about what life would be like as a father, he thought about Tick Dillon and McDermott, Jim O'Kane and then business. Even a light caseload has its burdens. Bills and insurance found their way into his thoughts, too.

The tracks led past his grammar school. He remembered that he and his classmates used to run across the field when the freight train would slug past during recess. It didn't matter what you were playing, who was winning, or even who you were fighting. When the train came by, you ran to it and shouted with tugging motions for the engineer to toot his horn. Gleason's legs weren't always fast enough to make it to the chain-link fence that separated the tracks from the playground, and by the time they were, the Boston and Maine had stopped passing. It was last scheduled to run the week of the Blizzard of 1978.

About an eighth of a mile from the bridge where Gleason and his boyhood friend, Jay Mangino, had smoked their first cigarette, and where Mangino had been struck and fatally injured by a car, Gleason noticed something on the bank just under the bridge.

As he got closer, he could see it was a young kid who had wiped out on his bike. Gleason ran under the bridge and over to the kid. The kid was crying.

"You okay?" Gleason asked.

The kid struggled to catch his breath. "No. I lost five dollars and my bike broke."

Gleason saw that the chain had fallen off. He turned the bike over and reworked the chain back onto the front and back sprockets.

"Trying to ride the rail?" Gleason said.

The kid nodded while he inspected the raspberry burn along his right arm and wrist. Then he said, "Yeah."

"That'll do it. Got plenty of wipeouts under my belt doing the same thing. Only we used to try to outrun the train."

Gleason thought he was relating. The kid showed no interest.

"What about my five dollars? My father's going to kill me. He sent me out to get some stuff."

The kid cried some more.

"You try back-tracking?" Just as he said it, Gleason considered the stream of wind whipping down the track line. If the five dollars existed at all, it had gone the way of the freight train. He reached for his wallet and found only three one dollar bills. There would be no afternoon coffee. He handed them to the kid.

"But I had five," the kid said.

"I did, too."

"Huh?" the kid came back.

"Nothing. Listen, kid, just look around. There's

probably five bucks worth of empties tossed along the tracks here. Collect those."

The kid showed no interest. He hopped on his bike and said before taking off, "You don't even have five dollars. You collect them."

Gleason turned and looked up at the bridge he hadn't walked under since Paul Mangino was killed. On the way back, he wondered why he had ever even cared about things such as freight trains and Irish farms.

He took a deep breath and walked under the bridge and back to his office. He thought about how Jay Mangino's mother used to say her son was a man of destiny. Like Teddy Roosevelt and Thomas Hardy, Jay Mangino was stillborn and pronounced dead at birth. The doctor placed him aside for a moment, and a nurse, who refused to believe that such a perfectly formed baby could be dead, slapped him on the back. Mangino coughed up a ball of phlegm and began breathing.

"WHO IS THIS lady we're freezing our nuts off for?" Nicky Jones asked the Big Man.

The Big Man just looked out the passenger's window and didn't answer his mate.

They were parked on Rice Street in North Cambridge. A breadcrumb's throw from where they were stood St. John's church, where Tip O'Neil's funeral Mass was held. Tip O'Neil—a local North Cambridge kid, the son of a bricklayer who used to clip grass for Harvard University during prohibition. During his duties once, he saw a privileged group of Harvard students openly drinking alcohol, and he became annoyed at their disregard for the law. He saw the incident as an opportunity to change things.

In the 1930s he lost his first political race for Cambridge City Councilor, but when he won his second time out—in the Harry Truman tradition—he became a man of destiny.

During the depression, armed only with a sense of humanity and a degree from a tiny university for poor kids called Boston College, Tip ran a campaign that pledged to fight for more work, safer conditions, and better pay. He went on to become the first Democratic Speaker in the history of the Massachusetts House of Representatives. And when he took over JFK's Congressional seat, he was eventually voted in as Speaker of the United States House of Representatives and became Washington's kingmaker before retiring in 1985.

At his funeral Mass, three former presidents, dignitaries from all over the world, Cardinal Bernard Law, and bi-partisan members of the House paid their respects, cheek by jowl with barbers, cobblers, firefighters, police officers, nurses, teachers, and his old North Cambridge buddies from Kerry,s Corner. Commentators said Tip could dine with kings or cabbages.

"I said, who's this bird we're freezing our ass off for?" Nicky Jones put out again.

"A Portuguese interpreter," the Big Man said.

"What the fuck do we want with the bird?"

The Big Man didn't answer.

A woman in her early forties was dumped off the bus onto Massachusetts Avenue and started up Rice Street.

"That's her," the Big Man said. "When she opens her door, that's when we grab her. Cover her mouth and direct her right upstairs."

The woman walked up the front stairs to the yellow Victorian and placed her briefcase between her legs before negotiating the door. It was dark. The Big Man and Nicky Jones pulled stockings over their heads and grabbed the woman just as she bent over to lift her case. She had no time to scream.

Jones stuffed her up the jogs of the staircase while the Big Man removed the keys from the door and put them in his pocket, then quietly shut the front door and the inner door that sealed off the front hall. Upstairs he pulled out a syringe containing eight milligrams of Versed and plunged it into the woman's arm, right through her camel hair jacket. She was out within seconds.

"Okay," the Big Man said casually, "flop her on a bed somewhere. See if there's one on the top level. She'll be out for the night and most of tomorrow, but if she stirs, put a small scoop of this in warm water and pour it into her. Don't take your eyes off of her."

"Wait a minute," Nicky Jones said. "I'm staying here with her?"

"Just until four-thirty tomorrow."

"What the hell is this stuff?"

"Valium."

"Why's it all powder?"

"I mash it up so it doesn't have any identifying numbers on it."

"I think she's dead," Nicky Jones said.

"She's not dead. She's out. Now calm the Christ down. This is a lay-up for you, for Christ's sake."

"How the hell do I get out of here, tomorrow?"

"Walk down to Davis Station and take the subway,"

the Big Man said. He held up a token pressed between his thumb and index finger with Eucharistic appraisal. "Here's a token. Don't lose it. And don't smoke while you're here."

"But I don't know how to take the subway. Which way do I go?"

"Inbound." The Big Man was descending the stairs. "Now don't fuck this thing up."

"Inbound?"

"Inbound."

Nicky Jones didn't like the set-up. He didn't like it one bit; yet he had no say in the matter. It'd been that way since he was a kid.

He looked down at the new token in his hand. If he tilted it in the light he could see the Big Man's thumb print.

TWENTY-SIX

IT WAS RALPH Waldo Emerson who first put down the words, "A foolish consistency is the hobgoblin of little minds."

More than sixty years ago, someone in Brick Village became convinced that the district line between the Brick Village District and the Liberty Heights District passed right down the center aisle of Sacred Heart Parish.

The folks from Liberty Heights were anything but from the ruling class; however, most of them were blessed with employment through the Great Depression, whereas most of the folks from Brick Village held themselves out as day laborers. Additionally, during the winter months, bread winners from the village stood in line for hours outside the Department of Public Works when snow was forecasted in hopes that they would be given a snow shoveling badge since they were distributed in limited number. If you were lucky, or had the connections, you'd be given a badge and this would entitle you to shovel out snow along the T tracks for ten cents an hour.

Even though wives would stuff old newspapers between their husband's inner and outer garments, pneumonia would still take its share.

The distinction between the working class people of Liberty Heights and Brick Village was negligible. Nevertheless, if people are willing, they will find the distinction. As a result, Brick Village sat, knelt and prayed stage right during services, and Liberty Heights stage left.

Today, the parishioners of Sacred Heart joke about the schism, but when it comes time to congregate, they do so accordingly.

Mrs. Gleason came up from the outer cellar with her hands full of baking potatoes. Joe was in the kitchen and tossed some bread crust to Wags.

"Did you get to Mass this morning?" Mrs. Gleason asked.

"I did. It was Father Foley."

"Was there a second collection?"

Gleason laughed. " I haven't skipped Mass since seventh grade, Mom. You don't have to quiz me on it. I enjoy going."

"What about Maria? She probably doesn't even know what side to sit on. Does she?"

Gleason shook his head. "I'm working on her, Mom. You can't make people go to church."

"Well, it wouldn't hurt. My God, even that G-D dog followed you into church once."

Mr. Sugrue walked into the kitchen, and Wags thumped her tail against the hardwood floor. Mr. Sugrue looked over at Joe.

"No work today?"

"It's Sunday, Gramp. I'm going to work tomorrow. I'm meeting Mr. Pettingill, as a matter of fact.

Tom Sugrue walked over to Wags and scratched her backside with the tip of his walking stick. Wags did a half roll exposing her belly.

Mr. Sugrue said, "Time wounds all heels."

Those without ideas often fall back on insults.

It was the chance of a lifetime for Gleason, and he knew it. Town Father Martin Pettingill was offering to give a young businessman in his community a chance to prove himself. Gleason was wearing a tie. Wags didn't bother to get up and greet Pettingill. She just lifted her head and sniffed the air.

"How have your mother and father been, Joseph?"

It was obvious Gleason was trying to get rid of his Boston accent all in one conversation.

"They're doing very well. Thank you."

"Good. I've known your parents a long time. Your father is salt of the earth. They did a good job with you two kids."

"Thank you."

Pettingill held up a cigar. "Mind if I smoke?"

"Not at all. I have one of those stand-up ash trays."

He offered Joe a cigar.

"No thanks, Mr. Pettingill." Gleason wanted one, but would feel awkward smoking around Mr. Pettingill.

Mr. Pettingill lit. "You really did a one eighty, Joe. Your mother never stopped believing in you. She told me how well you were doing, so I thought I'd see if I could throw something your way. I have quite a bit of rental property in Cambridge and Boston. You familiar with section eight tenants? I've been smothered with them ever since rent control passed."

"They got rid of rent control."

"Right. But I can only get rid of these animals through attrition."

"Yeah, but if these are section eight, doesn't the state come in with a good chunk of the rent?"

"It's not enough. I want them out, and I want you to find a way—one by one if you have to—to get them the hell out. Sooner as opposed to later."

"I'm not sure landlord tenant law is my field. It's a little too procedural for me, Mr. Pettingill."

"I'm not too concerned. We'll see how it goes for a while, and if you don't like it, no hard feelings. You just figure out how many hours you'll need to get on top of it and I'll give you a retainer. I'm sure once you get going, you'll be fine."

"That could be quite a bit. I mean, it sounds to me if you sit it out, attrition might be the more practical route."

"I think I'm hearing no from you, Joe."

"Not necessarily. I just don't think I'd have the wind for a file of this kind. Besides, I thought Frank Garland handled things for you."

Pettingill set his hands in motion. "Ha! Frank . . .Frank." He looked at Gleason as if he had uttered something naive and then said, "I'm still hearing no from you, Joe. This is a cash cow."

"It just doesn't sit well with me. I appreciate that you need to collect rent, but there are two sides to every valley. These people need a place to live, and I know you scooped up a bunch of property for a song when rent control first passed and the real estate market plummeted as a result. You knew the risk, and now that rent control's out," Gleason shrugged, "you have your own cash cow on top of God knows how many other cash cows you already have, and you want to use my ticket to hose off the crap. I don't think so. I'll tell my folks you pass on your best."

He looked around for the ashtray. It was right in front of him.

"You dumb Mick. And that fucking dog stinks,"

166

Pettingill said before leaving.

As soon as Gleason heard Pettingill's truck leave, he went into the bathroom and urinated. Afterward, he washed his hands and face with cold water, looked at himself in the mirror, and said to his reflection, "Nice job, you dumb Mick. Now go home and eat some fuckin' Cheerios." It came out with a Boston accent.

Later that day, while Gleason was smoking a cigar in his office and Wags was lapping up a dish of vanilla ice-cream, Gleason had this to say: "Don't worry, Wags. When you get down to it, fuck Pettingill, it's like being booed by Rangers fans."

❖

ATTORNEY LAWRENCE KENNEDY liked what he heard when a clerk from the Concord District Court tipped him off that Judge Jeremiah Plympton would be presiding as a visiting judge over the Big Man's case the day of pretrial conference. There wouldn't have to be any judge shopping. If he played the prosecutor right, this would give him an opportunity to button the matter up in one day.

Judge Plympton was adopted by a prominent Boston family but ran away when he was fifteen. He stayed out of trouble but not out of harm's way.

Not long after he ran off, he got a job working with the produce vendors at the Hay Market in Boston and learned from an old Italian fellow named Crispy how to trade produce, money, dice, and on occasion fists and whatever they held in them. At eighteen he talked a Jesuit at Boston College, Vincent Tacelli, into giving him a shot at an education. After graduating cum laude, Plympton did a few things in Korea that cost him his left leg, and in return got a pat on the back from an important incumbent for his trouble.

When he returned, the dean of Boston University Law School took a shine to him and let him in days, and he continued to work nights at the market.

After Plympton was admitted to the Massachusetts bar, he became a criminal defense attorney. Working at the market, he had built himself a good client base consisting of apple thieves, Irish tempers, and Peck's Bad Boy. The only phone he had available to him was located in a coffee shop next to Crispy's stand, and that's where his clients would call him.

With a name like Plympton, he ended up getting into the right Boston gentlemen's clubs, such as the Tavern Club and the Union Club. He didn't survive the keen scrutiny of the Somerset Club, however. It didn't break his heart—he had bailed out enough Irishmen in his early days to have Tip O'Neil and Governor Dever hand him a gavel to the East Cambridge Courthouse, and that was enough to lean on, Plympton figured.

TWENTY-SEVEN

TRIAL COURT OF THE COMMONWEALTH
DISTRICT COURT DEPARTMENT, CONCORD
DIVISION
CONCORD, MASSACHUSETTS

THE CONCORD DISTRICT Court finally got its metal
detector going, but the x-ray conveyer belt wasn't in oper-
ation yet. As a result, the officers working the door had
everybody empty their contents. This process caused a
backup of people trying to get in. Lawrence Kennedy and
the Big Man were early and didn't have to face the backup.
This gave them the opportunity to be well organized and
relaxed by the time Kennedy had session with the prosecutor, Jan Storrow, who, unfortunately for her, was running
a bit late that morning. It always shows.

The Big Man was unshaven. He wore an old black
blazer that was too small for him and, underneath, a green
denim shirt buttoned all the way up to his neck, with no
tie.

With a brown cap in his hand, he stood beside
Lawrence Kennedy in the hallway of the Concord District
Court as Kennedy tried to hash out a fair deal with the
assistant district attorney, Jan Storrow.

"Listen," Storrow said, "your man has quite the
record. I've read the report, and since this is his first OUI,
if he offers a plea, I'll drop the reckless driving, but he's
got to do school, court costs, twenty-five hundred in fines,
and a CWOF co-terminus with alcohol education."

"So you want a plea of guilty," Kennedy said.

169

"You said a CWOF was your pleasure."

"I did, but I was hoping my client wouldn't have to plea on this. He's not a citizen, and a CWOF is a plea of guilty. I'd hate to see that affect his status as an alien."

"Talk it over with your client."

"I can't. The interpreter's not in yet. You sure one's been ordered?"

Storrow flipped through her file on the Big Man.

"Yeah. They're apt to be late. I hope this doesn't go over to second call, Counselor."

"I'll tell you what," Kennedy said, "I'll fill out your offer on the defendant's disposition of terms on the green sheet and go over the terms when the interpreter gets here. If my client agrees, I'll have him sign it and submit it to the court. Get out of here early. I ask only that you soften the facts for me when you read them off to the judge."

Storrow nodded.

The green sheet is a Tender of Plea form. If, during pretrial conference, counsel for the defense and the prosecutor make a deal and the defendant agrees to it, the deal is put in writing on the green sheet and signed by the prosecutor and defense attorney and then the defendant. If a judge allows the deal and certifies the document in court, the deal is made and there is no need for a trial. The Commonwealth saves the expense of a costly trial and the defendant gets a reduction in charges. The defendant's Tender of Plea, however, is for all practical purposes a finding of guilty, yet the plea of guilty is not entered unless the defendant fails to satisfy the requirements set forth by the judge, either probation or otherwise.

Kennedy knew that the Big Man couldn't afford to be caught up in a trial. It could be pushed off for

170

months, but in between there would be motions, which would mean other court dates, and there would be affidavits in support of those motions, which would mean Kennedy would have to meet up with the Big Man. Senator Custance wanted the Big Man freed up, and it was Kennedy's job to see it through. The green sheet gave him a chance to end the matter as far as court was concerned, but that would mean drunk school and loss of license for the Big Man for at least forty-five days, and that could conflict with whatever Custance needed him for.

Kennedy wanted it both ways. He wanted the matter over with today and he wanted his client off without tendering the green sheet to the court, and he was going to have it both ways, too. And to boot, he was going to teach Storrow a little something about playing with city boys.

In addition to having four more cases to conference before court was in session, Jan Storrow had the satisfaction of thinking she had bested Kennedy into a tough plea, so she signed the green sheet and so did Kennedy. The Big Man did not.

"All right," Kennedy said after he and Storrow had signed the document, "I'll head down to the clerk's office to see if this damn interpreter has shown up yet."

The Big Man pretended not to understand and waited for Kennedy to pilot him toward the clerk's office.

An announcement came over the speaker stating that criminal matters would be in the third session. Mundi and Smith entered and took a bench seat in the back of the court.

Kennedy sat just below the balustrade assigned to counsel. The Big Man sat in the first row with his brown cap rolled up in his hands.

Kennedy got up and walked over to the table marked for the defense and pulled from a manila folder an appearance sheet, which attorneys are supposed to fill out and submit before handling a case in court.

He sat down and filled out the document, but did not submit it to the clerk, who sat directly below the judge's bench. The court officer was skinny, and his red tie reached only halfway down his mound.

Smith and Mundi were in the courtroom.

"Jesus. He could umpire with that tie," Mundi said.

Smith examined the court officer as he stood up to collate some files.

"Ties and minds can't be wide enough," she said.

Mundi smiled. "Who said that?"

"I did," Smith said.

"Good one. May I use it?"

"You may."

There was silence in the courtroom. "All rise," the clerk said with both hands pressed against the table in front of him. "Hear ye, hear ye, hear ye. All persons having anything to do before the Honorable Jeremiah S. Plympton, Justice of the District Court of Central Middlesex now sitting at Concord, within and for said District, draw near . . .Give your tenets and you shall be heard. God save The United States of America, The Commonwealth of Massachusetts, and this Honorable Court. Court is open. Please be seated."

Judge Plympton was seventy-three years old and wore no glasses.

"Good morning," the judge said after arranging

172

things the way he liked them, including his orange, black, and yellow-stripped Tavern Club bow tie.

His Honor's salutation drew a response from everyone in the room except the Big Man, who just sat there looking as confused as if he'd just arrived on Ellis Island.

The Big Man's file was passed up to the judge, and the court officer gave His Honor a moment to review it before calling the case.

"The Commonwealth of Massachusetts versus The Big Man."

Kennedy stood up and then motioned for the Big Man to stand. The Big Man stuffed his hands and hat into his blazer pockets, and when he approached the microphone in front of the balustrade, Kennedy motioned to him to remove his hands from his pockets and cross them in front of his person so that the judge could see them. This was a carefully planned gesture by Kennedy and the Big Man to show the judge how much Kennedy respected courtroom protocol and how much control he had over his client. Concealed hands don't fly with judges.

The judge nodded to Storrow.

Storrow approached.

"Good morning, Counselor."

"Good morning, Your Honor. May it please the court, Jan Storrow on behalf of the People. On the morning of November 21, Sergeant Susan Jacobs of the Lexington Police Department received reports from dispatch that a driver of a Century Buick was stuck on Wilson Farm property in Lexington. When she reported to the scene, she smelled a heavy odor of intoxicating liquor from the driver, later determined to be the defendant here before

173

us, The Big Man. In Sergeant Jacobs' estimation, The Big Man had been operating a motor vehicle while under the influence of intoxicating liquor, in violation of Massachusetts General Laws, Chapter ninety section twenty-four D."

"Thank you, Counselor. Have you and defense counsel had an opportunity to talk about this?"

"We have, Your Honor."

Storrow directed the court's attention to Lawrence Kennedy. She expected to hear Kennedy announce that his client plead the case. The court officer turned up to the judge and whispered something.

The judge said, "Has defense counsel filed an appearance?"

"Your Honor, may it please the court, Lawrence Kennedy, Boston . . . counsel for the defendant. May I approach the bench on an issue relating to Mr. Green, Your Honor?"

"Approach the bench, Counselor," Judge Plympton said while waiving him over.

"Mr. Green" is a code used in court to let the judge know that counsel hasn't been paid for legal services.

Kennedy said, *sotto voce*—in a whisper—"Your Honor, my client hasn't paid me yet, and, as you know, once I file an appearance with the court, he's mine."

"Does he have any money?" the judge asked.

"That's the thing, Your Honor. He doesn't have much money. I was going to handle this matter *pro bono*, but I anticipated resolving it this morning."

"I thought you and the People talked."

"We did, Your Honor. However, it was on the condition that an interpreter explains the terms to my client, and there's no interpreter here. Without the benefit of an interpreter, I can't in good conscience have my client sign away his rights when he doesn't understand English. Additionally, Your Honor can't certify that you read my client his waiver of rights and, further, that he understood them."

"What language does he speak?"

"Portuguese."

"Did you try to get co-counsel who could speak Portuguese?

"I did, Your Honor. I called Harvard Defenders, and they're closed until after New Year's. I called the Boston Bar and the Massachusetts Bar Association, and they don't seem to handle the off line courthouses. I'm the only one who would help this guy."

"So, hash out a discovery and make a date for motions and go to trial then. Maybe something will pop open for you on the co-counsel front."

"It's not fair to my client, Your Honor. He's here today in hopes that he can get back to work. We're ready to make a deal. He can't afford a trial and he doesn't qualify for appointed counsel either. He has a right to plea this out, and if the state failed to produce an interpreter, my client shouldn't be the one who suffers."

"Well, what does he do for work?" Judge Plympton asked.

"He's a fruit vendor down at the Haymarket. He's scraping nickels."

"Who's he working for?"

"Waltham and Cambridge Tomatoes."

The judge pulled his lobe and frowned.

"I hate those pikers, but I won't take it out on your

175

client, Counsel," the judge said to Storrow, "approach the bench, please."

Storrow came to the bench and stood next to Kennedy.

"Did the People order an interpreter for this case?"

"We did, Your Honor," Storrow said, "but she's hasn't shown up yet."

Judge Plympton said to the court officer, "Call the clerk's office and see if the interpreter has checked in."

While the officer was calling in, the Big Man just rocked back and forth, looking at the judge as if his life hung in his hands. Judge Plympton reassured the Big Man with a wink. The Big Man returned a confused smile.

"Nothing, Your Honor. Shall we hold it over for second call?" the officer said.

The judge shook his head.

"What did you two discuss?" the judge asked.

"Alcohol education, six-month CWOF, loss of license—if there's a hardship, I recommend a work license, court fees, victim witness fee, head injury, and $2,5000 fine," Storrow said.

"Okay," the judge said to Kennedy, "I believe you did your best to resolve this matter without the aide of an interpreter. However, in light of the fact that your client is getting free legal services—and you are doing this without cost to your client—am I right, Counselor?" Kennedy nodded. "—I'm awarding the People fines in the amount of one thousand dollars. Keep the green sheet, Mr. Kennedy."

Storrow dropped her jaw. "Your Honor, I'm con-

176

fident that on appeal the Commonwealth will—"

"I'll note your enthusiasm for the record, Counselor. The defendant can't waive his rights without an interpreter. Now, is the Commonwealth going to appeal my decision?" the judge asked. "When we could save the Commonwealth the expense of a trial?"

Storrow considered the four cases she had slated to advance that morning. The last thing she needed was to challenge the judge's wisdom on her first case of the day.

"No, Your Honor, the People don't wish to appeal."

"How long does your client need to pay, Mr. Kennedy?"

"Thirty days ought to be fine, Your Honor," Kennedy said. "Thank you, Your Honor," Kennedy nodded, "Mr. Clerk."

Kennedy and Storrow walked back to their tables.

The judge turned to the clerk recording the result. "Okay, court costs in the amount of $1000 to be paid by the defendant in thirty days. No plea entered." He looked at Kennedy. "Due no later than nine a.m., Counselor."

"Thank you, Your Honor."

"Pick up the order before leaving, Counselor. Well done," Judge Plympton said.

Kennedy waited for the order to be drafted by the clerk and directed the Big Man out of the courtroom.

Mundi shook his head.

"What was that you said about ties?" Mundi asked.

"Ties and minds can't be wide enough."

"Someone ought to tell the judge to get rid of that

bow tie," Mundi said. "What a way to run the fucking railroad."

"This is it," Smith said before getting up to leave.

TWENTY-EIGHT

By QUARTER TO ten, Kennedy and the Big Man were picking up coffee at the Back Alley Caf in Concord Center (the "Milldam") and then heading back to Boston on Route 2 East. Kennedy figured he could push things aside for a day or so after that one.

Joe Gleason had no such luxury.

SOMETIMES THE BEST cases are the ones you don't take.

"Do you want me to go through it one more time? Because I think I should go through it again."

"No, I have it, Chris. I'm just not so sure you need my services, that's all," Joe Gleason said. "Besides, I don't do patent law. It's a specialty. I can grab a few names out of *Lawyer's Diary* if you want, but I can tell you, it's expensive. They'll probably want money up front."

Chris Bishop tightened his lips and shook his head.

"I only trust you. I'm gonna use you. I should just go through it one more time. You see, every breakfast restaurant has potatoes—home fries, whatever you want to call them. That's not creative. Ya gotta have a niche, ya know. So what I'm talking about is fried sweet potatoes with each breakfast. You got your two eggs over easy, your bacon, sausage, ham—whatever, ya know. And then your bagel, wheat toast, seven grain, plain white, dark rye, light rye, pumpernickel—whatever, ya know. And then a slap of just regular potatoes? No! I'd slap down fried sweet potatoes. They're unbelievable."

"Can you cook?"

"Anybody can cook."

"Have you ever been in the restaurant business?"

"I worked dietary in the nursing home."

"You were a dishwasher in high school, Chris, for two months. You never made it past potato peeling when you were fired for doing beer funnels in the walk-in freezer and then squeezing some high school girl's Charmins."

"So, you're not gonna help me out?"

"I don't want to see you waste your money. Work in the field for a while and see if you like it. Restaurants all over are looking for help. Besides, if you go to a bank for a small business loan, they're at minimum gonna ask for a business plan and experience in the field."

"So, you can't help me."

"What do you want me to do?"

"Help me get going. Get this thing off the ground."

"I'm telling you how to get it off the ground. Get experience and get a business plan together."

"Yeah, well, I gotta work. I can't sit on my ass all day like a lawyer and write a business plan."

"So, what am I supposed to do? Give you money or something?"

"You're an asshole, Gleason. You selfish prick. You got your fancy law office and you forgot where you came from. I could've cut you in."

"You've got me nailed, Chris. You figured it all out. I'm a fuckin' millionaire hoarding money from all the working class heroes such as yourself. I won't give you a free ride, so I'm an asshole. I had to cross just as many lines as you did, only I didn't fuck it up along the way."

"Yeah, whatever, Gleason."

Chris Bishop stood up, turned, threw a fist through one of the windowpanes in Joe Gleason's door, and then slammed it on his way out of the office.

"That'll burn some bridges," Gleason said to himself.

While working a fragment of glass out of a miter joint, Gleason cut the palm of his right hand.

The words of Tick Dillon echoed through his office: "Sometimes you do more harm trying to help."

❖

"HEY," SMITH SAID, "it's eleven-eleven. That's a lucky time—make a wish."

Detective Mundi closed his eyes, laced his fingers on his lap, and said: "I wish—I wish—I wish I was a fish."

Smith burst out laughing.

"You're a Don Knotts fan?" she asked.

"Guy's the greatest. Next to Wayne and Stewart, he's really the last symbol of American innocence and idealism."

"No question," Smith said.

"One of my favorite movies is 'The Ghost and Mr. Chicken.' It's a great look at small-town America. Times were so much simpler then. I remember it as always being sunny then."

"Those days are gone, brother. I remember when I was little girl, I used to walk to school alone. I was five years old. And then about the time 'The Partridge Family' went off the air, a high-school girl in my town was kidnapped. The pig made her strip down and he took pictures of her right along the highway, believe it or not.

181

When the guy was changing his film in the camera, she took off and, in a state of panic, flagged down a car. A guy stopped and she jumped in. Couple of miles down the road *he* raped her. I remember after that, when I used to walk to school or play, whenever I heard a car coming, I would hide behind a tree or whatever I could find. The days of 'I'd like to buy the world a Coke' are over."

"I read somewhere that true liberty is the highest form of bondage," Mundi said.

"I wouldn't know," Smith said. "I wouldn't know."

TWENTY-NINE

It was twelve past eleven when the Big Man pulled up to the interpreter's house on Rice Street. He pulled out the keys he'd recovered from the door when he and Nicky Jones had sacked her, and then let himself inside. In the front hall, he found a temporary guest-parking permit and went back outside to put it on the dashboard of the car.

Upstairs, Nicky Jones was passed out in a chair next to the interpreter. The Big Man kicked his foot.

Nicky Jones wiped away his sleep in panic and said, "How'd you get back in?"

"I got the keys."

"What time is it?"

"Quarter past eleven."

"You're early. I didn't think you were coming back. I thought I was supposed to leave at four-thirty?"

"I thought I was going to lose my license, but I didn't." He looked over at the interpreter. "Did she see you?" the Big Man asked.

"No. She's been asleep. She stirred once, so I gave her some Valium in a cup with warm water, like you said."

"You were asleep when I got here. How do you know she didn't wake up at some point and see you before she passed out again?"

The Big Man removed a .38 from his coat and began attaching a silencer. When he was done, he released the safety and pointed it at Jones' head. Then he pointed it at the interpreter.

"Her or you? I could go either way," the Big Man said.

Jones shook his head and cursed his own ignorance.

"Does that mean you or her?" the Big Man said.

"It means her," Jones said.

He looked at Jones and then lowered the gun until it pointed at the interpreter's head. Jones closed his eyes. The Big Man lifted the gun, went over to the interpreter, and felt her neck. She was out cold.

"Come on, fuck it," he said. "Let's go down and make some breakfast instead."

"Make it here?" Jones asked.

"Sure, I'll clean up."

In the kitchen, the Big Man warmed up a long electric fry pan with a slab of butter on it and then placed four slices of bread individually on the counter. Next, he selected a small glass from the cupboard and pressed the mouth of it against the face of each bread slice until there was a circular hole punched in each one.

Jones went to work on the coffee and found a spare moment to skate the butter over the fry pan until it was all melted, and then threw on eight sausages. What he lacked in stakeout intelligence he made up in the kitchen.

"Put it on low or you'll burn everything," Jones said. "My fuckin' father used to do that. Turn the goddamn jets up as high as they go and burn everything when my mother was junk. Whole fuckin' apartment full of smoke. Burned everything and didn't have a clue, and then he'd kick the shit out of us if we didn't eat it. Sometimes if we did eat, he'd kick the shit out of us. The outside burned and the middle still frozen. And then

184

my mother'd wake up with no booze and a husband who couldn't hit it full speed anymore because he had soft serve for a prick, so she'd knock the shit out of us."

"Shut your fuckin' mouth," the Big Man said. "Sounds like the fuckin' 'Waltons' compared to where I grew up."

The Big Man took the four bread slices with the cup holes in them and laid them on the fry. He then took an egg, cracked it, and dropped it into the hole of one of the bread slices, and repeated the process for the remaining three holes. He also fried up the round pieces of bread punched out with the glass.

Just as the Big Man piled equal portions onto breakfast plates, Nicky Jones removed two raisin and cinnamon Thomas' English muffins from the toaster oven and buttered them. He lifted them over to the table and dropped the Big Man's share onto his plate.

The Big Man looked over the delivery and questioned it.

"What is this?"

"English muffin. Raisin and cinnamon."

"I know it's a goddamn English muffin, but my question is why do I get both tops?"

"I don't get ya," Jones said.

"Both tops. Both tops of the muffins. It's like one third the fuckin' size of the bottom. You got the two big halves of the muffins, you selfish prick. These are fork split. The top is always smaller than the bottom. You telling me you didn't notice?"

"I just fuckin' buttered the things and brought them over to the table, for Christ's sake. I didn't know weights and measures was gonna get involved. Jesus

185

Christ. Take mine—make a switch. Do what you gotta do."

The Big Man pointed a knife at Jones. "You're fuckin' cleaning up, you cheap bastard."

Upstairs, the interpreter forced her eyes open and began to stir. She felt nothing but blankness and yawned until she thought the skin of her lips would split open.

When her feet touched the floor, she expected to feel rug, but instead she heard the sound of her shoes clacking hardwood.

The Big Man and Nicky heard the noise. The Big Man wiped his face with a paper napkin printed with a rustic pattern, and rose from his chair.

The interpreter tried to stand up and lost her balance. Falling back onto the bed, she pulled the blanket up to her neck and passed out.

The Big Man entered the room, walked over to her, and felt her neck. He determined that she was out cold and then turned to leave the room, but before leaving he removed his gun, turned back, and deposited two bullets into the interpreter's head.

Jones was upstairs in time to see what happened.

"Come on," the Big Man said, "we have to clean everything."

When they were done cleaning, the Big Man put his gun to the back of Jones' head and pulled the trigger, and what was inside Jones' skull freckled the white wall before he slumped to the floor.

Out in the car the Big Man went over everything in his head. There was something he had forgotten. Something he couldn't put his thumb on. Shaking it off, he started the car and exited Rice Street taking a right onto Rindge Avenue.

The Big Man abandoned the car on the second level of the Alewife parking garage and took the escalator to the ground floor. He fished for his token and then remembered that he'd given it to Jones and had never recovered it.

NEXT MORNING JUDGE Plympton brought his mug with turtle figures on it to his lips and blew before indulging in a tiny sip of Postum. He lowered his hot mug of Postum and shook his head after reading the headlines of the *Herald American*.

"No wonder that poor bastard didn't have an interpreter," he said shaking his head. "Someone's out killing them all. Jesus, Mary, mother of God all mighty."

THIRTY

MUNDI PULLED A cigarette out from Smith's Winston glide pack 100's and put it behind his ear.

"That cat killed over in Cambridge, Nicky Jones, chummed with the Big Man," he said.

"CPAC's handling it," Smith said.

Crime Prevention And Control—"CPAC"—is the State Police's criminal investigating unit in Massachusetts, which investigates most of the homicide cases in Massachusetts.

"I know. You ought to get on the horn and see if you can find anything out from them."

"You think this has a connection to the Big Man?" Smith said.

"I know it does," Mundi said. "Just have to prove it."

Mundi left. When he turned the corner, he mashed up the cigarette he took from Smith and deposited its remains onto the desk blotter of the departmental pain-in-the-ass.

ABOUT A MILE and a half past the Colonial Inn in Concord Center, veering toward Carlisle on Lowell Road, is a patch of conservation land named the Old Calf Pasture. Just before the bridge that passes over the Concord River, there is a rutted tributary used to launch canoes, and it is accessible by car.

When the Big Man was done securing his car, he walked down a meandering path that followed the cuts of the river. About a quarter mile into the woods, he found whom he was looking for and spoke to him.

"One of these years I'm going to get the dog out here in the summer."

The man he was speaking to was the gunsmith he had met at Benson's diner in Wayland. The driver adjusted his glasses and exhibited a wan smile.

"You wanted four bullets," he said. "I got you six. You could have one in the chamber, but I didn't bother, considering your client might lack the manual dexterity. You said you liked simple."

The Big Man launched his eyebrows. "Good figuring. You got six bullets?" He sounded impressed.

"I did. You guys are so old fashioned. It's basically a stew: a mixture of a Browning, British-Lewis, and a pinch of an old Czech blowback. Silver tipped .22 caliber. The bullets will penetrate but in all likelihood not exit the target. They flatten on impact and make a mess of the target's inside. Oh, and by the way, it actually works."

The driver pulled out a small brown case about three and a half inches by six inches, unsnapped the top of the case, and removed the piece.

"You put it together just like an actual one. They're made to come apart so that they can fit in these pouches and be toted around."

The driver put the piece together and then unfolded a clean sheet of white paper. He handed the gun and the piece of paper to the Big Man and said, "Here, try her out."

The Big Man's face savored doubt.

"If it fires, it'll hit me right in the gut."

"It won't fire until I show you how to make it fire," the driver said with some pride.

189

The Big Man held the gun in his hands and felt it for weight.

"I got it less than a pound," the driver said.

The Big Man slid the piece of paper in between the two clamps of the gun and squeezed. When he was done, he pulled out the piece of paper and witnessed the perfect impression of a notary seal.

"It's even got the little Indian," the Big Man said.

"Look at the name I put on it," the driver said with plenty of enthusiasm.

The Big Man read it out loud. "John W. Booth . . .Massachusetts . . .Notary Public. How does it fire?"

"Not as difficult as I would have liked, but again, I'm keeping your client in mind." The driver took the seal from the Big Man. "The bottom plate is your rotating pan, which contains the bullets. Fires from an open bolt, so if the bolt goes forward," the driver stopped and elevated his shoulders and let them fall back into place before saying, "it'll fire a cartridge. See this small lever where it reads 'Slide Lock'?" The Big Man acknowledged that he did. "Slide it back and turn it clockwise as far as it will go. When that's done, turn the bottom handle of the instrument clockwise. The upper handle opens to your grip, the trigger folds out, and the bottom handle becomes your barrel. Accurate to about eight to ten feet, maybe fifteen if you're a good shot . . .or a lucky shot."

The Big Man gave it a feel. The driver could tell it felt awkward to him. "Shape and pitch of the grip are a bit funky," the driver said. "But, like I said, I kept it under a pound."

The Big Man nodded. "And it works?"

"Like the proverbial charm."

"Okay. Prime it and run me through it again."

The driver went through it again, and the Big Man handed him another four thousand dollars.

The Big Man examined his surroundings and said, "You know, I really have to get my dog out here next summer."

BEFORE SCREWING THE cap back onto the ketchup, an old woman lifted the bottle up to her face and cleaned the rim off with her tongue. The Big Man, witness to the event, neatly folded his napkin in disgust, returned it to the place setting, and marched out of the restaurant.

"I REMEMBER MOSTLY when we used to hang out on Thursdays," Gleason said. "That's when we had half days at school. It was different back then. Both our parents worked. We were like ten or eleven, and we were on our own after school from noon. Today kids have to be watched.

"Mangino was a smart prick. He figured out that when it started to get warm, the snow banks would melt and there'd be change by the parking meters that had fallen into the snow when it was high and would show up when it started to melt. We'd walk up town along the tracks, all the time thinking Bang Russell was following us. We knew he wasn't, but we'd act like he was, only neither one of us would admit we were acting—"

"Who's Bang Russell?" Maria asked.

"Some booze bag who used to light the meadows on fire all the time. He'd light his own house on fire too, until he killed one of his own daughters, and then they put him away. But even after that, we'd say he got out and was chasing us. We heard he died in dry out and we still pretended he was after us."

There was a long pause.

"I couldn't figure the guy. After it rained he would walk around and pick up the worms that swam out to the street and then put them back in soil. Sometimes we'd help him. Anyway," Gleason said, "Mangino and I would go down the tracks to the center and walk along Mass. Ave. in March and April looking for change by the meters. Sometimes we'd agree to pool the finds together and sometimes we'd agree we were on our own, but most of the time we'd help each other out if the other guy couldn't buy something like a *Mad Magazine*.

"We'd go down the farm sometimes. It was the first time I remember stealing something. A bag of caramels. I didn't even want the thing. And when I offered Mangino a piece, he didn't want any either. I figured if he ate it, I could eat it, and he knew that's what I was after—to have him condone the theft. Funny thing is, he was the one who used to steal the cigarettes. Like I said, he was a smart prick."

Maria rolled into her husband and pulled the comforter over both of them. Gleason's right arm rested over his forehead. It was some time before he lowered it into the warmth pressed against him.

THE TWELVE DAYS of Christmas rolled by. There was no sign of it slowing.

"The days are long and the years are short," Mr. Sugrue said to Joe Christmas Morning.

Maria gave Joe a cookbook.

Joe Gleason had Tony Vaccaro's grandmother, Mrs.

Sacco, make pillows for everybody and assured her at the same time that he was looking into that health proxy she wanted. Tick went back home to Cork for a couple of weeks, but no matter where the gang went, almost everybody agreed that next year they would have more spirit over the holidays. This year, things just came around too fast.

Next year.

THIRTY-ONE

JOE GLEASON WAS tipped in his law office chair, watching the snow and rain fall and thinking about taking down his wreath when the tires to Buddy MacBeth's flatbed cleaved the fresh blanket of slush outside the law office. Buddy alighted the cab with a burlap bag full of coal in his right hand.

Buddy was seventy-six and from ships-of-wood and men-of-steel stock. His father was Scotch-Irish and immigrated to Nova Scotia in the 1890s as a boy, and later became what used to be known in Boston as a "two-boat carpenter." In the 1920s, Buddy's father set out on another ship to Boston to do carpentry. There were many like him. They were known as "two-boats" because they took one boat across the Atlantic to Nova Scotia, and then a second boat to Boston to pretend they were carpenters.

"Could've dropped your plow for me, you cheap Scotsman," Gleason said.

"I drop my plow for no man who doesn't pay me up front, Joe. Always get it up front or you'll get it from behind. Got that goddamn stove going yet?"

"Just waiting for my Christmas coal. Late as it is. Come in. How much do I owe you?"

Gleason was reaching for his wallet and Buddy stopped him. Wags was up and took a few hearty pats from Buddy after Wags' smell test.

"No you don't, Joe. Forget it."

"Bull shit. Let me pay you."

"Put your goddamn wallet away."

"You sure?"

"Put your goddamn wallet away."

The old gent bunted the tips of his work shoes against the kickboard outside Gleason's front door to knock the snow and sand out of the treads.

"At least have a cigar and beer," Gleason said.

"I can do that," he said, spilling an ample amount of coal into the top belly of Gleason's stove. He had the honor of christening it for the first time that year.

They sat back in their chairs, each with a Miller long neck and a Churchill Partagas.

"When did you graduate high school, Buddy?"

"Forty-two."

"You join the service right after graduation?"

"Right after the summer my number got called up, and before I knew it, I'm on a plane to the goddamn Azores. I was looking through some stuff the other day and found I still have my short snorter."

"What's a short snorter?"

Gleason leaned with his stogy canted.

"Flying over the Atlantic was still a big deal back then. Hell, I crossed it less than two decades after Lucky Lindy. When Churchill signed one on his first flight to the States, it became the vogue to pass a dollar bill around and have everyone on the plane sign it. You had to keep the bill too, because if you went to a bar and claimed you were a short snorter and couldn't produce it, you had to buy everyone in the bar a drink."

"Jesus, you must've carried that thing around with you like it was your prick," Gleason said. "You were in the Air Force, weren't you, Buddy?"

"Forty-nine missions and crapped my pants in every goddamn one of them." He smoked and chased it with a swig of Miller High Life. "'The Rubber Check' was the name of our plane. Always came bouncing back."

"What were you?" Gleason asked.

"I was a gunner." He lamented over another swig. "Christ. No one wants to die anymore."

The telephone rang and Gleason scooped it.

"Joe Gleason."

"Joe, it's Tick. I've been arrested. They charged me with killing Jim."

THE WARRANT THRESHOLD

"ARE YOU ABSOLUTELY sure about that?" Mundi asked.

"I am," Smith said. "I'm ninety-nine percent positive. At least, that's what I read in *Readers Digest*, anyway."

"Good source. Won't take it on. What about a square?"

"No. A square will go through."

"A rhombus?"

"I'm telling you, only a circle."

"That's unbelievable. So the reason manhole lids are a circle is because if they were any other shape they could fall through." Mundi nodded his head in amazement.

"That's what I've been telling you for the last half hour," said Smith.

"Are you sure?"

"I'm positive . . .I'm pretty sure."

Madam magistrate approached.

"What do you need, Jack?"

"An arrest warrant from a neutral and detached magistrate."

"Whatta you got?" the magistrate and/or assistant clerk asked.

"On November thirtieth of last year, Patrick Dillon did, by means of a cigarette, unlawfully kill a human being, Mr. James O'Kane, with malice aforethought, in violation of Massachusetts General Laws, chapter two hundred sixty-five, section one," Mundi said and then told her how he and Smith had figured all this. She didn't seem impressed.

"Commonwealth requires more than just a totality of the circumstances, Jack. You know that."

"Is this an Italian thing, Mrs. Reilly?" Mundi asked.

"Don't let the surname fool you. I'm only Irish by injection."

She handed Mundi a blank warrant. He filled it out and then directed the pen in Smith's direction.

"Why me?" Smith asked.

"Because I may not be around. They'll kick the shit out of it. With all due respect, of course, for the late detective. And then they'll go ahead and kick the shit out of it."

When Smith had finished signing and dating the document as the complainant on behalf of the Commonwealth, Mrs. Reilly jumped off a phone call, signed it, stamped the date and time of issue, and then went back to the phone only to be further scooped on her Great Aunt Mary's, sudden—yet chronic—case of angina.

THIRTY-TWO

TWO YEARS AGO, BRICK VILLAGE, ARLINGTON, MASSACHUSETTS

UNDERNEATH THE SHEET of plate glass covering Attorney Sam Greenstreet's desk were no pictures of family or friends, just a yellowed, typed list of what he charged for wills and trusts. His office was on the second story of an old box-framed house known as the Town Conscience Building.

Joe Gleason was in a wooden chair watching his brother attorney pull on his morning cigar.

Mr. Greenstreet had his narrow frame tilted against the yellow pine casing of his office window overlooking Massachusetts Avenue. He was seventy-four years old.

The old lawyer saw something outside and said, "Come and watch this guy, Joe."

Gleason got up, stood side by side with Mr. Greenstreet, and looked out the window. He saw a man across Massachusetts Avenue whacking the engine of his new snow blower with a hammer. Gleason laughed.

"Don't laugh," the old lawyer said. "I have a feeling this one might ruin my coffee."

They watched the scene a little more and then sat down.

"What can I do for you, Joe?"

"I've got a chance to buy that old gate tender's shack down by the strip plaza, and I was thinking about hanging out my own shingle. I'd like to be a country lawyer."

"Whom did you work for?"

"Cutter and Dudley."

"I know, but whom, I say? You speak like Cutter and Dudley are actual people. It's a legal fiction. They don't have talent like you. They have resources."

"Lawrence Kennedy. I did mostly criminal law but also some litigation."

"Sounds like they had you marked as a trial attorney. How long did you work for him?"

Gleason hedged. "Six months."

Mr. Greenstreet sensed the hedge. "But how long as an attorney?"

"Four days."

"Is that it?" Mr. Greenstreet asked.

"Yeah. I know I'll make some mistakes, but—"

"Don't worry about mistakes. Sometimes they help you. There was a time when I relied on them. But still, do you think that's enough time? Four days?"

"I think so. I worked with a good number of contractors around town, so I have some connections. I think I'll get the business. It could lead to real estate."

"You'll get every contractor's nightmare is what you'll get. Every legal shit sandwich that comes down the pipeline." The old lawyer fit his cigar into his mouth and then tilted back in his chair with his fingers laced behind his head. "So, you worked for the great Lawrence Kennedy?" The question was put to him in such a way that Gleason knew he wasn't supposed to answer it. "Do you know what it means to be a canary in a coal mine, Joe?"

Gleason shook his head.

"They'd send canaries into mines to test whether or not poisonous gases were lurking. If the canaries died, the miners wouldn't enter."

199

"Tough to be a canary. At least they didn't die in vain."

"It would seem so."

"So, what are you telling me?" Gleason asked.

"Nothing, maybe. But maybe something you couldn't learn after four days. Forty, possibly, but not four." The old attorney hesitated before saying, "Let me tell you a story, Joseph. I worked as a medic during the Second World War, in Karachi, India, for a few months and then was sent to Calcutta for a year to do clerical work. In October of 1945, I was sent back to Karachi, and I decided it would be best to utilize the training I had received in the medical unit.

"One morning, not long after I arrived, there was an explosion. It was some distance from the building I was in, but the boom could be heard throughout the hospital area. The building actually vibrated. Presently we got word that a gasoline tank behind the mess hall had exploded when a GI, on his way to the mess hall, had thrown a cigarette away. It fell within range of the fumes and the whole thing blew up.

"There was a young Texan of Mexican origin . . .he had an accent . . .Gustave Velasco, who was near enough to the tank when it exploded to catch fire and was burned over two thirds of his body. He was brought into the hospital almost immediately and treated by doctors who were skilled in burn cases. Several days later he was moved to the section of the hospital where I was working.

"You should know that burns at that time were treated by wrapping the patient's wounds with Vaseline gauze. This method of treatment seemed to be effective at the time of the Coconut Grove fire, which took almost

200

five hundred lives. The method was later repudiated, but at the time it was considered a real lifesaver.

"It was obvious that Gustave needed special nursing. I had never worked with a burn case before, and I hadn't been told that a badly burned person emits a unique odor. Once you've become aware of it, you'll never forget it. Even the oxygen tent he was in didn't contain the smell. When you went off duty, the first thing you had to do was to take a thorough shower and change your clothes. The odor attaches itself to the skin and impregnates the clothes of anyone brought into association with it.

"Over a period of time, we could see new skin forming. As his condition began to improve, I had many conversations with him, and he told me he had a brother who had been killed at Anzio. Hearing what happened to him would be rough on his mother, back in Texas.

"The doctor treating Gustave was a Chinese doctor named King from Wisconsin Medical School. Later, Dr. King was transferred, and another doctor assigned to the case. The new doctor decided to strip off all those Vaseline dressings and re-bandage Gustave. When the dressings came off, the new skin came off with them, virtually flaying him alive. Infection was inevitable and set in almost at once. He was delirious part of the time, but I think he knew what had happened. He had been hospitalized from late October and now we were into early December. I wasn't there the night he died. In fact, I was kind of glad when I went off duty because I had a feeling he wasn't going to make it through the night.

"When I was leaving the states to go to India, I'd put some American soil in an envelope and put it in my

201

luggage. I said to myself, If something happens to me over there, if I can, I'm going to have someone sprinkle this on my grave so that I'll know I was buried in American soil.

"I still had that package in my bobo bag and figured my own time in India was waning, so there was no real likelihood that I would die there and need the soil for myself.

"Gustave was buried in a cemetery we'd set up just outside of camp. I sprinkled that soil on his grave and wrote to his mother in Texas, trying to make things as positive as possible.

"Gustave died on December 13, 1945. It was a Thursday. He was nineteen, and a bad decision took his life.

"Remember that his faith itself was not burned, not severely so, anyway. Not his. I never did meet the person who blew him up."

"I thought you told me not to worry about mistakes," Gleason said.

Mr. Greenstreet just tightened his lips and raised his eyebrows.

There was a moment of silence and then a knock came on the outside door. Mr. Greenstreet got up and let the caller in.

"What can I do for you?" the old lawyer asked.

"I just bought a new snow blower and the thing doesn't work," the man said.

"You try choking it?"

"I tried everything and it won't go."

"You didn't meddle with it yourself, did you?"

"No," the man said. "I just bought it. It should start right up."

202

"So, what do you want me to do?" the old lawyer asked.

"I want you to sue them and get me a new one; one that works. This is consumer fraud."

There was a pause from the old lawyer. He ran his hand through his thick, white hair and gnawed at the stub of his cigar. "Well, better get it up here so I can take a look at it."

"The blower?"

"No," the old lawyer said. "The hammer you weren't hitting it with."

When the man left, Gleason laughed and said, "That didn't ruin your coffee after all."

The old lawyer folded his hands in front of his face and looked down at the sheet of plate glass covering his desk with no family or friends underneath it all. His shoulders bowed, he said, "It did more than you think, Joe."

That afternoon, Mr. Greenstreet's four o'clock coffee grew cold after his heart made one final push for life and his troubles passed.

THIRTY-THREE

THE ARREST

"WE JUST CALLED you in here for a statement, that's all," Smith said to Tick Dillon. "Give you a chance to tell your side of things."

Tick didn't say anything.

"Here's the form for voluntary statements. If you want to make one—make one. It says right on it you're not under arrest."

"I'm not under arrest?" Tick asked.

"No."

"But it would be better if I cooperated?"

Smith turned her hands. "It's been my experience. We just need to know what happened to Mr. O'Kane. It's all bullshit, I'm sure."

Up until that moment, Tick had presumed he'd been summoned to the station concerning the death of McDermott. When he heard it was about O'Kane, he was only too happy to volunteer a written statement, since it was an accident. When he finished, he handed the statement to Smith. After reading it, she told him he was under arrest and read him his Miranda warnings.

After Tick was processed, Smith said to Mundi, "What do we do now?"

"You see, the McDermott one is going to be tough to prove. But it gives the connection to the O'Kane since Dillon was probably afraid O'Kane was going to talk. Throw the McDermott on the lap of the district attorney's investigators and let the prosecutors throw it in as motive for murdering O'Kane. It may not be one they can prove,

204

but it's a story that'll make sense to a jury."

GLEASON WAS ON the horn to Lawrence Kennedy right after he got the call from Tick.

"Lawrence, you mean that about working together on a file?"

"Of course, Joe. What's up?"

"A friend of mine just got busted for murder and he called me. These guys think I can handle everything, but I'm not competent to handle something this big."

"All right. Bundle up a file, get in here and we'll move. This guy have any money?"

"I know he has six thousand."

"For me to even touch Superior Court is twenty-five, but we'll grab the six and he'll come up with it. Does he have family?"

"He's got a girlfriend and she's pregnant."

"Excellent. If she's ready to calf, the last thing she'll want is for the daddy to be in jail. She'll come up with the money. They borrow it. They always do."

"I'll be over as soon as possible," Gleason said before hanging up the phone.

"Sounds like trouble," Buddy said.

Gleason shook his head. "This is going to be a long life, Bud."

"You can take off, Joe. I'll make sure the fire goes out and see to it that Old Wags gets home."

STRETCHING HIS RIGHT leg under his desk, Mundi switched off the power strip that fed his computer with his foot. Smith came over and sat on some papers lying on his desk.

205

"Head out for a binge?" she asked.

"I can watch."

Smith was silent.

"You know," Mundi said, looking at the blank computer screen, "when we first got these things, I said to heck with this, they're useless. I was so stuck on the old way. But you guys, younger guys like you, come along and just blow us away. And that's not all. I mean, this thing grew on me like a partner, ya know?"

"Yeah, those things have feelings."

"I know. My great-grandfather was a brush maker and he had all these great tools. He used to make box kites too, I guess. When we were kids, my brother and I used to bring them outside and make tree forts or whatever the hell it was we did. We ended up losing most of the tools along the way. My father would kick the shit out of us. I have an old ball hammer and a small anvil left and that's about it. Other than that the toolbox is empty. Nope. Not like the old days."

"Yeah, well, we new guys never had a chance at the old ways," Smith said, "and you don't know it, but we wish we did. You had both; the old way and a chance to see it evolve. That's something we'll never have."

"This is it. This is my last day. I've had it . . .I'm tired." Mundi slid open his bottom draw and pulled out the cover to his computer monitor. "I'll just drop this pall over my friend here and we'll hit the road. Stapler's yours."

"Thanks," Smith said.

"So where am I watching you get stewed?"

"Twenty-First Amendment."

"Remind me. I think I left one of my kidneys

206

there."

"You won't need your kidneys tonight, Detective. Tonight's going to be just like the old days."

"Good. It's been a long time between drinks."

TICK DILLON CAME up with fifteen thousand dollars, and Gleason talked Kennedy into accepting that as a retainer. Tick was arraigned at the district court level, and after being indicted by a grand jury, he was held over to Superior Court to be arraigned there for the first-degree murder of James O'Kane.

❖

GLEASON WAS SITTING on an oak swivel at Cutter & Dudley in Boston examining the facts of Tick's case with Lawrence Kennedy. In particular, the facts and circumstances surrounding the actual arrest of their client.

"The police had an arrest warrant for Tick, Joe," Kennedy said.

"Right. It seems they did everything by the book. Tick's girlfriend consented to the search, and since their room was used by both her and Tick, she could consent to the search. They knocked and announced too."

"The search didn't turn up much. I'm not worried about that. It's the way in which the arrest was handled."

"What do you mean?" Gleason asked.

"Are you familiar with "Mass. General Laws Annotated," chapter two hundred sixty-eight, section twenty-two?"

"I'm not." That was one of the reasons why Kennedy liked Joe. If he didn't know the answer, he said so.

"It states, in a nutshell, Joe, that an officer cannot willfully delay in the service of an arrest warrant except in exigent circumstances when they fear for their own safety or the safety of others. It's actually punishable by a fine of fifty dollars."

"What does that do for us in this case?"

"They called Patrick down to the station, and this detective Smith told him that he wasn't under arrest. She got a statement out of him when she already held the arrest warrant. She willfully delayed the service of it, and therefore, any statement she obtained from Patrick is fruit of the poisonous tree. We'll file a motion to suppress his statements, and without his statements, we may have grounds for a motion to dismiss."

"So this could work," Joe said.

"In theory, Joe, but a judge won't likely bang a dismissal on those grounds. But all we need is that little grain of sand to turn into a pearl and break the prosecution down. You want to handle the arraignment?"

"Can I handle it?"

"Absolutely. You have to get your sea legs sometime. He's being charged with a capital crime, so they have to read the indictment and then he'll plead not guilty."

Gleason shook his head. "Man, Superior Court. On the district level, we're just processing this stuff."

"Get to know the rules of evidence, Joe. There's no way around it on this level."

Gleason looked out a window, which overlooked the activity on Newbury Street. He said after some reflection, "Okay. I'll head into the lock-up tomorrow and have a chat with Tick before his arraignment. I'll do it, but you have to come with me."

"Absolutely, Joe. You'll do fine."

Joe took in a strange look from Kennedy and, against instinct, just shook it off.

❖

"WHAT WAS IT like when you first found out you had cancer?" Smith said to Mundi.

Mundi drew a long breath and held a drill bit up to the light. Then he said, "Doctor's telling me all the things I had to do. Setting schedules, tests, diet—whatever. And I'm just looking at this guy saying to myself that he hasn't a clue. I mean, I'm too busy for all that shit to be running back and forth. So I'm just yessing him to death so I can get the hell out of there so I can get back to the office. Well, he picks up on it and tells me to go and then call him in a couple of days after the shock wears off.

"Then it hits me on the way back to the station. It was something I didn't even know I had read, but I guess it somehow got into my head. When the doctor was talking to me, he was waving my chart in front of me and I read my profile from the lab work. 'Fifty-two year old male.' That's me. That's what I am. No matter who you think you are, you're just a nobody when it comes down to it.

"For some reason I thought of an old chest of drawers I had as kid that smelled like cedar. Then I cried."

He found the right size drill bit, inserted it into the throat of the drill, and tightened it with the chuck.

Smith said after he plugged in the drill cord, "I fixed your toothpaste for you this morning."

"Fixed my toothpaste?" Mundi said.

"Yeah. You squeeze it all over the tube and now that it's near the end, you couldn't get much out, so I fixed it."

"How?"

"I lined the bottom against the counter and pulled so all the toothpaste was forced to the top."

"That's just wonderful. Thank you."

"You're very welcome."

Mundi handed her his belt. "Hold this taut, Smith."

She held the belt as instructed.

"That good?" she said.

"Yeah."

Mundi drilled a new hole into his belt strap reducing it to a twenty-nine inch waist.

"Good," he said. "Now my pants won't be falling down. Cancer isn't going to get a new belt out of me."

THIRTY-FOUR

6:48 AM

It was January 23. Tick was remanded to a holding cell on the fourteenth floor of the Superior Court in Cambridge, and Joe was getting ready to head in for the arraignment.

"How do you feel?"

"Okay, but I'd feel a little better if Cagney were looking over me. I'm not sure it was a good idea to take the mirror down."

"Just remember you did it for God and country," Maria said.

"I thought I was doing it for you?"

"Same difference."

Joe smiled, lifted Maria's hair with his hand, and gave her a kiss on the forehead.

She closed her eyes, and when she opened them, she said, "You can't wear that shirt, Joe."

"What do you mean? It's brand new."

"I know it's new. It still has the fold marks in it."

"So? It's new."

"You have to get it dry cleaned or at least iron it."

Gleason looked down at his shirt. "But it's new. Jacket and tie will cover everything."

"You're impossible."

Gleason jumped into the bed next to his wife. "Listen, I have everything worked out. In five years we'll be out of here."

"Where are we going?"

"To Ireland."

"Ireland?"

"Yeah. I've been looking into it. I met an old man who told me everything I need to know about raising cattle."

"You're serious about this?"

"Absolutely. The only thing I have to do is learn to smoke a pipe like the old man."

"And," Maria said, "make enough money."

"Right, but I'll get the pipe thing down first."

Maria hooked her right forearm across her head and lamented, "What the hell did I marry?"

Gleason kissed her elbow. "Maybe just a good old fashioned dreamer."

"With a men's regular," Maria said.

"I'll be seeing you."

❖

7:15 AM

TOM SUGRUE SLURPED his morning tea and said to his grandson, "No work today?"

There were no lights on in the kitchen to lift the winter's darkness. Joe switched them on and said, "I'm working today, Gramp. I told you, I'm going to court. A friend of mine is in trouble, and I'm helping him out."

"A friend in need is a friend indeed. Courage, brother, do not stumble, though you pass the dark at night. There is a star to guide the humble. Trust in God and do the right.

"Trust no party, trust no faction, and trust no leaders in the fight. But in every word and action, trust in God and do the right."

"Some day I'll write that down, Gramp, but not today. Today I'll just have to take it with me up here,"

Gleason said, pointing to his temple with his right index finger. He patted his grandfather on the back and said, "Thanks, Gramp."

❖

7:23 AM

GLEASON STOPPED BY his office and went through a punch list to make sure he had everything. He was shaking and couldn't eat. His mouth was dry and his throat seemed bruised.

At his desk he said a quick prayer. He felt a little better and decided he'd force down an orange. Before working on the skin, he peeled off the blue sticker and stuck it to the plastic frame of his computer.

Before leaving his office he threw up the orange.

❖

7:48 AM

FROM ROUTE 2 East, Joe went past the Alewife Brook Parkway and over the John "Gus" DeLoria Bridge, and went straight until the traffic pushed left around the Stanley Teeven Memorial and kept pushing him straight into the gateway to Harvard Square.

John Lennon was singing on the radio that it would be just like starting over. Just weeks before the contents of a hand gun were emptied into Lennon's chest, killing him, Lennon had donated bullet-proof vests to the New City Police Department to show his gratitude to America for being granted permanent alien status.

At a stop light just outside Harvard Square, Gleason looked through the passenger's window and saw the back of the bronze statue of John Harvard, erected on a tiny slope of grass strapped in granite curbing, keeping watch over what he started.

7:56 AM

REVA SMITH WAS in before her shift. She looked over at Mundi's computer with the cover on it and told herself that it was still early.

To pass the time, she began reading in the paper about the events that led up to the trial of Julian Hill, the two hundred and fifty pound ne'er-do-well who raped and murdered Senator Custance's six-year-old daughter, little Jackie Custance.

❖

8:05 AM

MIDDLESEX COURT, SUPERIOR COURTHOUSE, 3RD DISTRICT, CAMBRIDGE

ON THE FOURTEENTH floor of the Courthouse, a tall, thin court officer stepped off an elevator leading to the holding cells and began his feeding. In the lunchroom across from the elevator, a handful of court officers argued about whether or not the puck had gone in the net or had hit the goal post.

The tall court officer got what he needed from the icebox and walked by the common office containing the surveillance screens.

From the large holding cell, a new head tried to get a peripheral view of the portal.

The court officer slid Julian Hill the sandwich and milk through the service opening of the green bars, and then took the elevator back down to Courtroom 6B of the Superior Court.

8:11 AM

JOE GLEASON TRAVELED down Broadway Street past the Department of Transportation and MIT, and just before he ran into One Broadway, he took a left onto Third Street.

Parking was killing him.

He took a right into the ALL DAY PARKING and pulled up to the attendant's shed.

"Nine, Rockafella," the attendant said. Gleason handed the attendant nine ones. "Put the slip on the dashboard," the attendant instructed, "and don't take up two spaces with your sled, Man."

6:32 AM

THE NEWS REPORTERS parked their mobile units along Second Street and hoofed it up to the front of the district courthouse on Thorndike Street across from the Bulfinch Building.

❖

8:15 AM

SENATOR RICHARD J. Custance had no comment and, in a fashion F. Lee Bailey might have envied, he pushed a throng of news reporters aside to prove it to them. The automatic doors slid open, and he helped his wife through.

At the top of the stairs a security guard had them remove everything from their pockets into a plastic container and Mrs. Custance sent her purse through an x-ray conveyer. Mrs. Custance stepped through the metal detector and it sounded. She was instructed to walk up to a guard and spread her arms. He waved a paddle over

215

her front and then told her to turn around. The process extended to the curves of her body and there was still doubt in the guard's mind. When he finally cleared her, he waved the Senator on and repeated the same scrutiny on him.

The guards were well aware of who the Senator was and were indifferent to his importance.

❖

8:14 AM

SMITH WAS STILL reading the headlines about Julian Hill when a jaundiced Mundi came up behind her and asked, "Who was the police officer we spoke with in Lexington?"

"Jacobs. Susan Jacobs," Smith answered. "Thought you were done with this place?"

"I am," Mundi said. "But remember what Jacobs told us about the Big Man?"

Smith shook her head.

"About the Big Man's booze. He bought it in Concord with a stack of fresh crispies. The Big Man always carries mint bills. Another one of his quirks. Gimmie the paper."

Smith handed it to him.

"Senator Custance of Concord, Democrat," Mundi read to Smith. "What does that tell you?"

Smith tapped her desktop. "Nothing."

Mundi just looked at her and said, "Nothing? The cop in Lexington was thorough. She's a good cop. What was the Big Man doing in Concord? Why are all those reprobates putting bets on the death penalty going through the state senate?"

Smith's index fingers were on her chin. Her eyes

widened.

"Maybe Custance is changing his position on the death penalty."

"Maybe he's doing more than just that, Detective. Maybe he's gonna pull the trigger."

"Right," she said. "If that fat, bogus creep, Hill, did that to my kid, I'd pop him first chance I had."

"Think so?"

"Know so. Should we call ahead?"

Mundi thought about it. "It's your ticket. But dropping dime on a state senator on a hunch may be fatal to a budding career."

Smith shot up from her seat and walked around. She went over to the water jug with her coffee mug and filled it. When she came back she said, "Not dropping dime may end a budding career, too."

"Like I said, it's your call."

"I need a coffee."

"We can stop by the IKOW on the way."

Smith said, "What's the IKOW?"

"The Italian Kitchen On Wheels. Parks right on Third Street."

Smith threw back her water and slammed down her mug. "Screw the IKOW, let's go."

THIRTY-FIVE

8:17 AM

ON THE CORNER of Third and Thorndike, a Cadillac stopped to deposit an average-size man wearing black gloves and carrying a dark brown leather attach case. Without shutting the door, the man walked over to the sidewalk abutting the Superior Courthouse and placed the case between his legs. The January thaw, which the Native Americans had called Squaw Winter, had arrived. The man unbuttoned his topcoat, partially exposing a pin-striped Chester Barry suit and a conservative gray tie with a Windsor knot.

The man adjusted his glasses and ran his thumb and index finger over his mustache before picking up the case and facing the automatic doors leading into the courthouse. With confidence, he entered, and at a steady pace went up the stairs and flipped the attach case onto the x-ray conveyer. Next, he reached into his breast pocket and removed an attorney's bar card to show security.

"Thanks for the bo-bo."

"Right on in, Counselor," an officer working the entrance said.

The alarm sounded and the officer working the metal detector paddle just went through the motions over the counselor.

The officer working the x-ray belt was going side to side in a swivel chair, working on something between his teeth with his tongue.

"You got a notary seal in there, Counselor?" the officer said, referring to the attach case.

"Yes, I do. That's right, I do. You're one of the few people ever to catch that," the counselor said.

"Okay. Go ahead." The officer leaned back, clasped his hands behind his head, and put his tongue back to work on whatever was stuck in his teeth. There was some silent appraisal. Being on the job, he was trained to notice the little things.

On the sixth floor, the counselor winked as he walked past Senator Custance, went into the men's bathroom, and entered the handicapped stall. Moments later, the Senator followed.

While in the stall, the counselor took the notary seal out of the attach case and showed the Senator how to convert it into a gun. The Senator's hands were shaking and sweating all over it.

The counselor said, "Calm down. Are you familiar with the set-up here?"

The Senator hesitated before saying, "I'm not."

"Okay. They won't walk him down the hallway. There's a couple of holding cells right behind the jury box. There's a door. The officer will walk him right through the door that leads him into the courtroom. Your best chance is to tap him just before the officer sits him down. You may not have time to put this together, so leave it the way it is. It's ready to fire."

"I'm so scared," the Senator said.

"Fuck 'im. Good luck, Senator."

❖

8:21 AM

JOE GLEASON WALKED down Third Street and went through the drill entering the Superior Courthouse.

He stopped in the snack shop to the left of the

219

front lobby and picked up a bag of potato chips for Dillon. When the elevator rang, he stepped into it and pressed the button to the fourteenth floor. Just before the doors closed, Mundi stuck his hand in and prevented them from shutting. He and Smith jumped into the car, and Smith poked the button for the sixth floor.

❖

8:21 AM

THE TALL THIN court officer opened Julian Hill's lock-up and maneuvered him down the gray portal into the elevator. Inside the elevator, he locked him in behind a metal grate and keyed the elevator to the sixth floor.

The elevator lowered to the lock-up behind Courtroom 6B, where the court officer placed the defendant in a small cell to await the beginning of the day's proceeding.

❖

8:21 AM

THE SENATOR AND his wife were sitting in the first row of Courtroom 6B.

"I have to head out to the washroom," Senator Custance said to his wife.

"You were just there."

He wiped his fleshy hands on the knees of his trousers and said, "I have to go. I have to go."

The Senator was out in the main lobby of the sixth floor wiping the sweat off his hands onto his suit jacket. He remembered his handkerchief and then pulled it out of his coat pocket and wiped his forehead.

A court officer with some manila folders in her right hand came out from behind the swinging doors marked COURT PERSONNEL ONLY and started for

220

the main lobby. The Senator saw her approaching, and his blood quickened. He began turning side to side like he was going to run, and the court officer took in his behavior.

"Can I help you with anything, Sir?" she said.

He didn't say anything. He just stood there, staring at her. Everything seemed to echo in his head. As she reached for her radio, the elevator doors opened and startled the Senator. He went to his inside pocket, pulled out the gun, and shot the court officer, hitting her in the left shoulder. Courtroom doors pounded open almost as soon as the shot thundered, and a team of court officers in clean white shirts charged the lobby.

Smith called out, "Senator, drop the gun!"

Mundi stuck his foot in the door, exposing his leg to the Senator's line of fire, and with drunken bravado, Smith hopped off the elevator car into the hallway with her .38 drawn.

"Senator, drop the gun!"

Senator Custance fired erratically into the elevator and hit Mundi in the leg. Mundi was thrown back, and Gleason took hold of him and spun himself around so that his back, not Mundi's, was facing the lobby. Before Smith could place a shot into Custance's shoulder, he fired a shot into Gleason's back. The elevator doors closed and it started for the fourteenth floor.

Gleason fell to the floor and scowled as the tug of the car went into his back. Mundi held Gleason's head and breast in his arms, and Gleason stared at the lights at the top of the car. They seemed to flicker on and off, as if feeding from stuttering jolts of electricity. He looked down at Mundi's leg and said, "You're bleeding."

"I'm okay. What the hell did you try to save me for? I'm dying, for Christ's sake," Mundi said.

Exhaling, Gleason said, "How the hell was I supposed to know that?"

The bullet in Gleason's back was taking noticeable hold.

"Hang in there, kid. Keep your eyes open."

"There's so much more to do."

"What's your name?"

"Joe Gleason."

A shadow of Gleason's blood spread along the linoleum floor of the elevator. He looked up at the recessed elevator lights, and they seemed to be turning black. Black and round like Cagney's eyes staring down at him.

"We all got plenty to do. Just hang on for me will ya, Joe?"

Mundi's leg felt frozen.

Gleason let out a long exhalation and passed out just before the doors opened to the fourteenth floor. Mundi glanced at his wrist and noted the time before the car descended back to the sixth floor.

The court officers had formed a circle around the Senator and were telling the crowd to keep back. Ambulances were ordered. They didn't know how many. Three at least. Photographers ignored the court officers' instructions and pushed toward the Senator.

Smith was waiting when the doors opened.

"How bad is he?" Smith asked Mundi.

"I don't know. Get an ambulance, for Christ's sake."

"Shit."

A few members of the press rushed the elevator. Smith jumped on, punched the close button, and the doors shut before they could film the situation.

Mundi was still on the floor with Joe in his arms. He removed his watch and handed it up to Smith. "Take this, Reva."

She just looked at him.

"Take it," he said.

The door reached the first floor and opened. Before noon, the scene was processed.

8:23 AM

THE OLD BLUE car was bucking up the hill past the Gleason's house. Wags had dug herself a nest in the hemlock bark mulch built up around the rhododendrons out front. When she saw the blue car going by, she climbed out of her bed and started lumbering up the hill.

By the time Wags climbed to the crest of the hill known as Mount Independence, the old blue car was nowhere in sight, but Wags continued, still convinced that it was Joe's car.

❖❖

THIRTY-SIX

8:27 AM

THE LONG, SLEEK Cadillac was waiting on the corner of Third and Otis Street for the counselor. The counselor opened the door, stepped into the back seat and said, "Without a hitch."

"Everything in?" the Big Man said.

"It is. I don't think your man has what it takes, but the bottom line is, we remain true to our word."

A pause.

"Interesting to see how this plays out," the counselor added, and then brushed something off his topcoat. "Whatever way, press is going to play it right off the boards."

The Big Man hesitated before smiling at the counselor. He cocked his right ear to take in the full sound of the sirens.

"That's why I like you, Al. You never fail me with respect to the little things."

The stretch coasted over the Charles River Bridge and then dropped Al off near the old Charles Street Jail.

Al collected five thousand dollars for his role as counselor.

"If this thing starts to flake," the Big Man said, "you may want to use this to disappear for a bit."

"Five thousand," Al said. "I should've been a lawyer always." He looked over at The Beacon Hill Pub and then ran his eyes over his watch and added, "Early," before the Cadillac hiccuped on toward Government Center.

"You know," the Big Man said to the driver, "by the time everyone gets paid, it just isn't worth it. We have to charge more. Deep down, I'm an old softy."

The driver pretended not to hear. A chauffeur should never have good hearing.

❖

7:00 AM

BEFORE GLEASON WENT to court that morning he was sampling ties under the supervision of his wife.

"Does this tie match?" Joe asked.

"Everything but the stain," Maria said. "The knot would make a nice throw pillow. And what's with the white socks?"

"My shoes will cover them."

Maria smiled. "You're worse than ten babies."

"Just one more thing," Joe said. "Should I stop, drop, and roll if I suddenly catch on fire in court?"

"Yes. Just don't cause a scene," Maria said.

"What would I do without you?"

"You'd be a one parish gypsy."

"I thought I already was?"

Maria shook her head. "I was wrong. You're on a mission to be a good father."

"I know who the real one parish gypsy is," Gleason said.

"Who?" Maria asked.

"Buddy MacBeth. Maybe the last of his breed. Do you know what a short snorter is?"

"No," Maria confessed.

"It's a dollar bill everyone on a plane crossing the Atlantic would sign during World War II. Buddy has one."

225

Maria tried to look interested. Gleason looked over at the windowsill where he put his flat of tomato starters and covered them with a small pane of glass. He walked over to inspect them up close.

"A couple have sprouted already," he said. "It's been only four days. Hope I didn't start them too soon."

"Go to work," Maria said.

Gleason kissed her on the forehead. "I wish I could go with you this morning. I'm worried about you driving."

"I still have another three months. It's just an ultrasound. I'll bring you home a picture of the baby."

"I can see her already," Gleason said looking into her eyes.

9:33 AM

"WOULD YOU LIKE to see the picture of your baby?" the doctor asked.

Maria cradled her stomach with her right arm and took the photo with her left hand. "Can you tell me what we're having?" Her face was glowing.

The doctor smiled. "I can tell you what you're not having, Maria."

"Joe's going to be so happy," Maria said.

"Of course," the doctor said.

2:48 PM

TRIAL COURT OF THE COMMONWEALTH DISTRICT COURT DEPARTMENT, WALTHAM DIVISION
WALTHAM, MASSACHUSETTS

THE PROSECUTOR WALKED into the criminal clerk's office on the first floor to update the clerks on the latest buzz.

"Hey, that lawyer shot today over in Cambridge was Joe Gleason."

"Who was Joe Gleason?" the assistant clerk asked.

"You know him. He was the guy what drove the old blue shit box with the Canadian flag license plate."

"Oh, yeah. I remember that guy. Is he dead?"

"I don't know."

A short pause.

"Why did he have that license plate?" the assistant clerk asked.

"I don't know, but Bobby Orr's from Canada."

"Was Derek Sanderson from Canada?"

"The Turk? I think so. I think Ken Hodge was from England, of all places," the prosecuting officer said. "I remember it like it was yesterday when I read in the paper that Pie MacKenzie was so hammered one night that he ripped off a motorcycle from a Boston Cop and drove it through a barroom window."

"What barroom was that?" the assistant clerk asked.

"I forget."

"I thought you said you remember it like it was yesterday?"

"Ask me about yesterday. I'm talking about when the 70s were still the 60s."

"Those were the days. For some of us. I got lost in Belmont the other day on some private road and saw a hippy bus with one of those old blue fish stickers on the

227

window parked in the same driveway as a Range Rover," the assistant clerk said before whirling off with a stack of files.

❖

NEXT DAY

Time wounds all heels.

AT MASSACHUSETTS GENERAL HOSPITAL, a nurse pressed the toe of her shoe on the pedal to a small trash bin, and when the lid said "Ahhh!" she dropped a paper cup into it before leaving Mundi's room.

Smith was standing over him with her arms folded. "I guess that Gleason fellow is in pretty tough shape."

"Is he going to make it?" Mundi asked.

"I don't know, Jack. He's tough. Like you."

Mundi worked some moisture up to his mouth. "I rode with the kid in the ambulance. He promised me a homemade pillow from some old lady he knows. I mean to collect it."

Smith put her hands in her pocket and said, "I met with a gent from CPAC this morning. I got a look at the Nicky Jones file. The Big Man's chum executed in Cambridge."

"Something turn up?" Mundi said.

"Yeah. A token. They found one on Jones in his pocket. I remembered you told me that the Big Man likes to ride the subway."

"And?"

"I told them what you told me. It was mostly smudged, but they got a few whirls of a thumb print."

"The Big Man's?" Mundi said.

Smith nodded. "Enough to put him behind the pipes for life, Jack."

Mundi smiled. "Too bad we don't have the death penalty." His face grew warm, and he felt his eyes swell. "I'm not going to let a cancer take me. I'm just not going to let it happen. I owe the kid that much."

Smith reached through the cold, chrome bars of the metal bedrail and gripped his bloodless hand.

"Rocky Raccoon does live in the end, Detective," Smith said.

"I know that now," Mundi said before resting his eyes.

THIRTY-SEVEN

TONY VACCARO WAS eyeing a slope of scrub.

"We're gonna take that hill," he said to the high school drop out. "We're gonna take that hill and turn it into a patio."

The high school drop out waited before responding.

"That's right. We're gonna take that goddamn hill."

"Right. We're gonna goddamn take it."

"It's going down, Sarge. We can't do the work of ten men, but we can do the work of five."

"Lock and load," Vaccaro said. "We gotta take that hill. But first we get a coffee and visit my grandmother. You gotta learn to relax in this life. Not everything's about money."

❖

196 DAYS AFTER THE SHOOTING
MIDDLESEX COURT,
SUPERIOR COURTHOUSE,
3RD DISTRICT, CAMBRIDGE

ON BEHALF OF Patrick T. Dillon, Lawrence Kennedy filed motion after motion with supporting affidavits signed by the defendant, Patrick T. Dillon, under the pains and penalties of perjury.

There would be no deal. Tick wouldn't take a plea. With all that went on, both the prosecution and the defense knew that this was a good one to bring before a jury.

In August, Kennedy's summation on Patrick T. Dillon was mostly about an attorney named Joseph C. Gleason. The prosecution objected on four occasions, but Kennedy could tell a story, and the jury didn't like the Commonwealth interrupting a good story about a good guy.

The story had a sad ending. It was about guy who believed in justice, in the values his parents had taught him, in his wife, and in the future of his baby girl.

Kennedy told the jury about a young attorney who spilled his blood on the floors of the Cambridge Courthouse, defending a friend he believed in his heart to be innocent. The jury didn't like it when the prosecution objected to that.

Joe's utterance after he was shot, echoed in this sacred courthouse, as Kennedy told it. It was one of pain. Not just physical pain, but the pain of not knowing. The jury could never give the horrific events a happy ending, but the good guy didn't have to take a bullet in vain. Let him hear the words "not guilty." Let him know he did his job. They could finish it for him. That even in the wake of these tragic events, justice would triumph. That had to mean something.

After deliberating for three hours, Madam Foreperson announced the words: "Not Guilty."

Kennedy took his left hand off Tick's right shoulder and gave him a hug.

COUNSELOR KENNEDY LED Tick Dillon down the granite treads of the Cambridge Courthouse and shook his hand before stepping into a black Lincoln Continental sweeping by to collect Kennedy. It was off to a late lunch and an early happy hour.

At the happy hour, Kennedy learned that his judgeship was approved. The firm knew about it first and wanted it to be a surprise. He was happy and didn't really know quite what to say.

The August sun was bright, and Dillon had to squint his eyes. He was deciding whether to go up or down Third Street. Either way, he was on his feet—when he wasn't on a stool.

FROM ACROSS THE street, Reva Smith looked at Dillon and then consulted the wristwatch Jack Mundi had given her.

Two young lawyers were walking past her, and she listened to the heavy one tell it the way he saw things.

"That's where you want to be," he said to his buddy while pointing at the courthouse. "On the criminal side of things. That's the sexy part of law."

"Yeah, screw pushin' real estate forms," his buddy said. "It's a waste. You don't even have to be a lawyer to do the crap we're doing. We should start our own practice. See some action."

"Yeah, but you can make some quick cash just doing title searches, and you don't even need insurance."

Smith looked at Dillon heading in the direction of Kendall Square. He stopped in for one at the Third and Charles Grille and bumped into an old friend who bought him a drink. It didn't help. The friend's nods didn't help. No contrition. Tick would live a long death.

Smith thought about her drinking. She wouldn't try to hide it anymore.

Tom Sugrue stood up at the end of the Gleasons' driveway as the old blue car lurched up past the Gleasons' house. He was wearing a sleeveless T-shirt. Weeds had propagated in the cracks of the driveway, and he'd been extracting them one at a time while on his hands and knees.

Wags, in her twelfth year, crawled out from the nest she had dug around the root ball of a rhododendron, as she noted the old blue car rumbling up Mount Independence.

The old blue car stopped in front of Gleasons' and Wags showed her delight as Joe Gleason stepped out with a dog biscuit in hand.

"No work today?" his grandfather asked.

"No work today, Grampie. I got a little girl to take care of."

"I do what I do because I like what I do."

Joe smiled, and Wags was already searching for a second helping.

With his thick hands Tom Sugrue clutched crab-grass and spurge. The elderly man turned and started off for the back yard. He would purge the unwanted growth invading the foot of the Virgin Mary statue he'd erected nearly seven decades earlier.

THIRTY-EIGHT

DETECTIVE REVA SMITH stood with her right shoulder propped against the jamb of the door connecting the break room to the squad room.

Louie Armstrong was singing in the background, "What a Wonderful World."

"Good to have you back. What are your plans today?"

Mundi was filling out the Refill Order Form to his agenda calendar. "What'd you have in mind?"

"Thought I'd go out and save America. Could use a hand."

"I'm your man. That Dillon fellow got off on the O'Kane murder. Maybe we can look into that McDermott fellow who got murdered in Brighton."

"Good place to start." Mundi swallowed and said, "Smith?"

"Yeah."

"Something I've been meaning to ask you."

"Yeah?"

"Why do you have the Italian flag hanging above your desk?"

Before she could answer the departmental diplomat approached. "What's going on?"

Smith and Mundi communicated.

"!"

"?"

"Mundi says the reason the '33' is on the bottle of Rolling Rock beer is because that's the same year that the Volstead Act was repealed by the Twenty-First Amendment. I say it's because some prognosticator who worked for Rolling Rock during its inception knew that Larry Bird would be such a good player and simply wanted to honor his number."

The departmental diplomat expressed his confusion. "Volstead Act?"

"Prohibition," Mundi said. "Prohibiting the manufacture, sale, or transportation of liquor."

"Oh," the departmental diplomat said. "I'll get back to you tomorrow if that's okay. Okay?"

"That's marvy," Smith said as she sipped her carrot and parsley cocktail.

"Tomorrow," Mundi said as he leaned into the homemade pillow lining the back of his chair. "Tomorrow will be just fine."